AWAKENED BY HER BEAR

BLACK RIDGE BEARS BOOK 5

FELICITY HEATON

First printed October 2021

First Edition

Layout and design by Felicity Heaton

THE BLACK RIDGE BEARS SERIES

Book 1: Stolen by her Bear

Book 2: Rescued by her Bear

Book 3: Saved by her Bear

Book 4: Unleashed by her Bear

Book 5: Awakened by her Bear

The Black Ridge Bears series is part of the Eternal Mates World, which includes the Eternal Mates series, Cougar Creek Mates series, and the London Vampires series.

Discover more available paranormal romance books at:
http://www.felicityheaton.com

Or sign up to my mailing list to receive a FREE vampire romance ebook, learn about new titles, be eligible for special subscriber-only giveaways, and read exclusive content including short stories:
http://ml.felicityheaton.com/mailinglist

CHAPTER 1

Bronwyn shook as she stared at the screen of her laptop. It blurred, the words swimming out of focus as her mind struggled to comprehend what she had just read. She jumped as another email joined the chain, this one containing a link. Her hand trembled as she moved it to the touchpad, shifting the pointer to the link, and she swallowed hard as her finger hovered, debating whether to click it.

Another email appeared, this one containing a single ominous sentence.

We know you're there, so open the link, Bronwyn.

Her gaze leaped up to the tiny lens of the webcam, her heart rushing in her ears as she realised they were watching her. Someone had hacked into her laptop and hijacked her webcam, and now they were sending her sick emails about her brother.

Another email joined the chain.

Open the link.

She drew down a deep breath, attempting to steel herself. It did nothing to calm her nerves. She glanced around the small café, thankful that it was empty, and grabbed her laptop, bag and coffee and moved to one of the window tables, where she was as far as she could get from the baristas.

Bronwyn slumped into the low armchair and set the laptop down on her knees, angled the screen back so she could see it, and rifled in her bag for her earbuds. She had come here to make use of the free Wi-Fi to catch up on her emails and her favourite TV show, stealing some quiet time for herself, away from the pride. Only at the top of her list of unread emails had been one with a single word for a subject line.

Andrew.

Curiosity had made her click it and fear had kept her staring at it long after she had finished reading the explicit text that had detailed all the ways they were going to harm her brother if she didn't do as they wanted.

She glanced out of the window at the sultry evening, part of her wishing she had never come into Whistler and the rest of her thankful that she had. If Andrew was in trouble, then she had to help him. He was her only immediate family, and while they didn't see eye to eye at times, she loved him deeply and would do anything for him.

Bronwyn pushed the headphone jack into the socket and clicked on the link.

An online meeting site popped up and she clicked again, accepting the invite, her stomach churning as she tried to mentally prepare herself, aware who had her brother.

Archangel.

The fiends had taken him again, must have captured him when he had been returning from his latest trip to Vancouver, one he had made every month for the last few years, always leaving her on the first and rolling back into the pride around a week later. Or two weeks as it more frequently was these days. The time he spent away from her was growing longer and longer, and it worried her.

Andrew had grown bored of life at the pride and she was starting to get the feeling he preferred being in the city, or maybe being away from her. Since he had matured, he had been less interested in hanging out with her, had begun to view her as a nuisance, one who cramped his style and put off the females he wanted to impress.

A picture opened on the screen, stuttered as the image shifted, growing pixelated, and then it became clear.

She gasped.

Andrew.

He kneeled on the concrete floor of what looked like a containment cell, held behind a thick wall of glass that was far too familiar, haunted her dreams most nights.

Archangel *had* caught him.

The hunters had captured her brother and were holding him in a compound again.

Her heart ached and fear swamped her as she stared at her brother where he leaned forwards over his bare legs, his dark head hanging close to them, his arms bound behind his bare back by thick metal cuffs. Crimson patches stained the pale concrete in front of his knees.

Bronwyn reached a trembling hand out and brushed her fingers across the screen, blinked away the tears that blurred her vision as she fought to make herself believe what she was seeing.

"Say hello to your sister, Andrew." A haughty female voice came over the microphone, her accent Canadian.

Andrew lifted his head, his golden eyes bleak as he stared at the owner of the voice.

Bronwyn covered her mouth with her other hand, her fingers shaking against her lips as his gaze shifted to the laptop someone was clearly pointing at him. Bruises ran across his cheeks below his eyes and there was a thick gash over the bridge of his nose. Blood had run from it to mingle with the crimson that drenched the lower half of his face, completely covering his mouth and chin.

"Bastards," she breathed and glanced at the baristas, wanted to scream at the bitch who was holding her brother and had been torturing him by the looks of things, but knew that if she did she would draw their attention. They would want to contact the authorities and this whole situation would only get worse for her—and for her brother. She tried to hold it together so they didn't suspect anything was wrong, but it was hard as she stared at Andrew, as rage kindled in her veins and had her close to growling and flashing her fangs as they dropped. "Let him go. He's done nothing wrong. We're not a threat."

Archangel were meant to only target non-humans who were a danger to mortals, but the noble cause was a front. The heart of Archangel was rotten, filled with vile hunters who sought to make money off her kind or get their kicks by watching shifters rip each other apart in the cages of their underground arenas.

Places like the one she and her brother had been held in after Archangel had raided their pride.

None of her kin had been a threat to humans. They had been peaceful, happily co-existing with them. Archangel hadn't cared. The leaders of the local secret arena had needed fighters, fresh blood for the cages, and had taken more than a dozen of her pride. Only she and her brother had survived long enough to escape.

The image moved again, blurring as someone turned the laptop around, and then a middle-aged blonde female filled the screen, dressed in black fatigues and wearing a cold look in her dark blue eyes.

"We will let him go, Bronwyn, providing you do as you're instructed."

Bronwyn barely leashed the urge to flash fangs at her, wanted to ask what would happen if she didn't, but knew in her heart what the answer would be.

They would kill him.

"What do you want?" Her voice shook as she asked that, fear getting the better of her as the female turned the camera back to her brother.

That fear jacked up as she saw he wasn't alone now.

A big dark-haired male was in the cell with him, gripping Andrew's chestnut hair and pulling his head back. She swallowed thickly and shook her head as he caressed Andrew's throat with the flat of a short blade, his brown eyes locked on the camera, a sick glint in them that said he wanted to hurt her brother, was hoping that she would try to resist or wouldn't do as they ordered.

"I just want you to do something for me. That's all." The female voice came over the video of her brother. "If you don't."

Bronwyn lurched forwards as the male nicked her brother's jaw with the blade and a thin rivulet of crimson spilled down his throat, a wild need to stop him flooding her, making her desperate.

"Please. Just tell me what to do." She cursed herself, hated how quickly she surrendered the fight. She had never been the defiant one out of her and her brother, had always been the one who sought the peaceful route out of a conflict, unable to bring herself to hurt another, even if it was emotionally.

Which is why she only felt more terrible when the female spoke.

"You would have received a cell number in an email. You're going to dial it and make contact with the one who answers it."

Bronwyn's stomach twisted in a tight, painful knot and she pressed her hand to it, sure she was going to throw up. She would do anything for Andrew, but this female was asking too much of her. She couldn't swap someone else for her brother, wasn't sure she could live with herself if she did such a thing, placing someone else into his position.

But one look at him was enough to have her denying the softer part of her, the one that didn't want to hurt someone like that. If she didn't do this, then her brother would be the one suffering, and they might even go as far as killing him. She couldn't live with herself if that happened either, and the pain she would feel would be far worse than if she did as the hunters wanted, subjecting someone else to their wretched plans.

The male in the cell with her brother lowered his blade, poising it against Andrew's throat. Andrew tried to lean back to stop the male, but the hunter tightened his grip on his hair, keeping him in place. The weak growl that left Andrew's lips was enough to have her giving up the fight again.

She sagged as her strength left her. "Fine. I'll do it. Just stop hurting him."

The image moved again, blurring and then revealing the female. She smiled at Bronwyn.

"You'll make contact with the shifters and get them both to agree to meet with you. We will call again in due time with the next set of instructions." The cold look in the female's blue eyes didn't mask the sick satisfaction the huntress was feeling as Bronwyn's eyes slowly widened.

The female had made it sound as if her task was bringing in one shifter and now there were two?

A need to shake her head rolled through Bronwyn, the thought of luring not only one but two shifters to their demise causing bile to rise up her throat. She tamped down the urge and tried to silence the whispers in her mind, ones that asked her where this would end. If she brought this female the two shifters, would she then send Bronwyn out for more, and more, forcing her to keep bringing her fresh blood for her arena?

"If you tell anyone about this or fail to follow instructions…" The female turned the camera back towards her brother.

He screamed as the male hunter plunged the blade into his bare shoulder.

"Andrew!" Bronwyn lurched towards the screen, her heart lodging in her throat as the hunter twisted the blade and blood ran in a thick stream down her brother's arm. "Please. Stop. I'll do whatever you want."

She glanced at the baristas, found them staring at her and locked her gaze back on the screen. She was running out of time. They would call the police soon.

"Miss?" The brunette female barista came to the end of the counter nearest her. "Something wrong?"

Bronwyn shook her head and snapped, "I'm fine."

Her gaze leaped back to the screen, her heart sinking as she stared at her brother.

She had to do this.

She could hate herself for it later, once it was done, when she had to live with it for the rest of her life. If it meant saving her brother, she would do anything.

The haughty female voice echoed in her ears. "Make the call, bear, and if you even think about warning them, then your brother is dead."

The video ended.

Bronwyn stared at the image that remained on the screen, brushed her fingers over her brother as she ached inside, feeling hollow and cold to the bone. She could do this. She had to do it.

She frowned as the screen changed, revealing an option to download the video, and found herself drawn to the link. She clicked it, saving it to her hard drive, and then closed the browser.

Stared at the latest email.

It contained a number she didn't recognise.

Bronwyn grabbed her phone from her bag and added the number to her contacts, closed her laptop and hurried from the café, not slowing until she was a good distance away from it. The air was still warm as she moved through the streets, numbed to her soul, resisting the urge to cry. She paid no heed to everyone who looked at her, keeping her head down and hoping they wouldn't stop her to ask her what was wrong.

She crossed a car park and headed through the thin strip of trees to the stony shore of Blackcomb Creek and stilled there, breathing deep of the cooler air, fighting for the strength to make the call. It was them or her brother.

Bronwyn stared at the water rushing before her as she dialled the number, shut down the softer part of her that had her wanting to find another way to save her brother, because this was the only way. She was going to do this, and for the rest of her life she was going to have to live with the knowledge that she had subjected two other shifters to the hell her brother was going through.

But it was them or her brother, and she had to choose Andrew.

Her hand shook as she brought her phone to her ear, her mouth drying out as she listened to it ringing at the other end. Her heart thundered, beating so fast she felt sick and dizzy as she waited. Maybe they wouldn't answer. Maybe she could tell the hunters that and they would let her brother go. She laughed at that, a mirthless chuckle. Maybe she needed to stop deluding herself. The hunters wouldn't let her brother go, not unless she gave them what they wanted.

The line crackled as the ringing stopped.

"Hello? Who's this?"

Oh gods.

Tears welled in her eyes, blinding her, and she covered her mouth as her brow furrowed.

Oh gods, no.

She shook her head, a chill sweeping down her arms as she recognised that deep, masculine voice, as she realised what the hunters wanted her to do. She couldn't do this. She couldn't.

"Hello?" Maverick's baritone was more of a growl now, losing all lightness, and she could almost picture how he would look, his silver-grey eyes gaining a sharp edge as his black eyebrows knitted hard, forming that little crease between them that had always been a permanent feature.

Except for the rare times he had smiled at her.

It had been so long since she had heard the voice of the grizzly who was like another brother to her together with Rune, one who had protected her countless times and had taken good care of her when they had all been held captive by Archangel.

The urge to tell him everything that was happening was strong, had her afraid to speak in case she accidentally blurted it. She cursed Archangel again, despising them for making her do this, unsure whether she could go through with it.

"Anyone there?" Maverick said.

"Maybe it's a prank call." Rune's voice was distant, but she caught it, wanted to cry and scream at the same time as she thought about handing these two bears over to the hunters.

Maverick snapped, "Who'd prank call me?"

Rune muttered, "Someone with a death wish?"

Maverick huffed at that.

Bronwyn couldn't believe she was going to do this, but it was her brother's life on the line. She denied the urge to tell Maverick everything, to trust that he could help her. The hunters would kill her brother.

"I'm hanging up."

She panicked.

Whispered, "Maverick?"

Silence.

And then his deep voice rolled over her.

"Pooh Bear?"

She huffed now. "I told you to stop calling me that."

He cleared his throat. Sighed. Not a sigh of exasperation, or any emotion she could decipher. He always had been skilled at hiding his feelings. But if she had to name the feeling behind his sigh, she might have called it relief. Or something akin to gratitude, as if he was glad to hear she was alive.

They hadn't spoken since the raid that had freed them from captivity, had gone their separate ways thanks to her brother, but she had missed him and Rune every day of the twenty years they had been apart.

Rune said, "Who is it?"

Maverick's deep voice warmed her and irritated her at the same time. "It's Winnie."

"Little Winnie the Pooh?" Rune sounded as surprised as Maverick did and then his tone darkened. "What's she doing calling you of all people?"

"What the hell's that supposed to mean?" Maverick growled back at him. "What's wrong with Pooh Bear calling me?"

Bronwyn smiled at how familiar all of this was. Rune had always been more fatherly towards her, had always done his best to shield her from the darker side of life at the compound. Maverick had always wanted to toughen her up.

She wished he had managed it as she growled, "I'm not a cub anymore. Stop calling me Winnie the Pooh or Pooh Bear!"

"What's wrong, Bronwyn?" Maverick sounded serious, the hard edge to his voice making it easy for her to picture how his face would be set in dark lines, his grey eyes bright with a hunger for violence.

It would have scared most.

But gods, she melted at the way he said her name, feelings she had been suppressing for decades rolling up on her to break over her, catching her in the swell of them. It was Maverick on the other end of the line. Maverick those bastards wanted her to hurt, trading him for her brother.

Maverick.

She clutched the phone as if she were holding on to him.

Maverick who she'd had the crush to end all crushes on. A galactic-sized crush. She could remember every time they had come into contact, their skin brushing, whether it had been intentional or accidental. She could remember every smile he had given her. They had been rare, but she had cherished every one.

Because he had only ever smiled for her.

A need to protect him warred with a need to protect her brother and she was torn between them again, just as she had been the night they had escaped, unsure whether to choose him or Andrew.

Her heart or her blood.

She squeezed her eyes shut, sending tears slipping down her cheeks, and drew in a shuddering breath to steady her nerves, to give her strength.

Because she had to do this.

She had no choice.

She lined up the words and forced them out.

"I'm in trouble."

CHAPTER 2

Maverick clutched the phone to his ear, unable to believe it was little Winnie calling him. Just the sound of her voice roused a fierce protective instinct in him, and that instinct had transformed into a compelling need to go to her the moment she had announced she was in trouble.

He stared at the world outside the window of Rune's cabin, restless with a need to move, to do something as his friend stared at his back. He could feel the bear's desire to know what was happening and could sense the curiosity of the female Rune held balanced on his thighs, but he couldn't bring himself to turn away from the window, couldn't stop himself from staring into the distance, all of his focus on the female at the other end of the line.

Winnie sounded the same as she always had—softly spoken, too gentle to be part of the seedy, violent world of the underground arena where they had been held.

Too innocent to be exposed to the things that had happened there.

To be exposed to him.

His heart thundered, drumming at a fierce pace as he fought the need to leave the cabin, battled the restless urge to go to her even when he didn't know where she was.

Little Winnie needed him.

His bear side prowled, shifting back and forth, wild with a need to go to her, goading him into surrendering to it.

He tamped it down, tugged on the leash and brought it to heel, because he was done letting it control him, knew better than to surrender to it every chance he got now. Those days were behind him.

"What kind of trouble are you in?" Maverick said, blood rushing in his ears to fill the silence.

Rune helped. "Winnie is in trouble?"

The big bear set his wolf mate aside on the crisp beige couch when Maverick looked at him, his pale blue eyes flicking to her, concern shining in them as he stood. In the weeks since Callie had come into his life, Rune had been making one hell of an effort when it came to sprucing up his cabin, making it fit for a female. New couch. New drapes. New bed. Maverick barely recognised the place.

Rune strode over to him and pressed close, his arm rubbing against Maverick's as he leaned his head towards the phone, listening in on the call.

"What's up, sweetheart?" Maverick willed her to answer him.

No matter how low her mood had been, or how fierce, she had always responded to him calling her that. She had always talked to him whenever he had been gentle with her.

She was quiet for a few seconds more and then sighed. "I don't want to talk about it on the phone."

He frowned at that, a seed of suspicion taking root in his mind, one he denied because he was just on edge, still struggling to cope with the shock of answering the phone and hearing her voice when he hadn't heard a word from her in twenty years. It was transporting him back to the compound, flooding him with memories of that place, pushing him off-balance to the point where he was starting to regard everything with wary eyes.

Hell, even the peaceful stretch of pale grey pebbles and green grass between him and the other three cabins on this side of the creek came under his scrutiny, his gaze seeking anything out of the ordinary. He tracked Saint as the big dark-haired male crossed from his cabin to the left, one that stood with its back to Maverick, heading towards the two cabins to the right of the clearing that had their sides to him and their rears to the thick pine forest that covered the foothills of the mountains.

"You can tell me anything. Just tell me what's wrong," Maverick said and waited.

Holly bounded towards Saint, caught up with him and looped her arm around his, her black hair swaying as she turned to her mate. Saint bent his head towards her and said something, and then looked ahead of them again, to the cabins. Lowe and Cameo were hanging out on the deck of Knox's cabin, talking to him and Skye. Probably planning tonight's menu. Saint had said something about a belated welcome party for Callie.

Life at Black Ridge was getting busier by the day, and Maverick had thought it would disturb him, but he had found part of him welcomed the addition of the females.

In particular, Rune's female. His friend deserved to find happiness after everything he had been through. Maverick rested a little easier knowing Rune was taken care of, that he had a future to look forward to, and the love of a good female.

He switched his focus back to the female on the other end of the line, growing impatient as she refused to answer him.

"I… I'm sorry I bothered you." She sounded defeated, upset, and fear swept through him, cranking him tight.

"Don't hang up." Those words burst from his lips, ripped from him by the thought that he might never hear from her again if she did. "I'll meet you. Ah… I can meet you at…" He looked at Rune and then at the others as Saint and Holly reached Knox and Lowe and their females. An idea struck him. "I'll meet you at The Spirit Moose. I'll text you the address."

Skye owned the bar and it was a place he could control, one where he would feel safe and less on edge, looking for trouble in every shadow.

"Thank you." Gratitude shone in her voice, softening it, easing some of the tension from him and he relaxed as he loosened his death grip on the phone. She sighed. "It's been a long time."

Maverick muttered, "It has. I remember you like it was yesterday though. Little freckled-face Winnie the Pooh, always hanging out in our cell, brightening the place with that smile that refused to fade."

Giving him hope that there was a better future for him out there somewhere.

Her tone hardened. "I'm not a cub anymore. I'm not little freckled-face Winnie the Pooh. I'm an adult now."

It wasn't like her to be so snappish. Whatever had her running scared had to be serious.

He tried to hold back his sigh as he thought about her, but failed.

"You'll always be that girl to me." He wasn't sure what he had done wrong when she met that with a huff that spoke volumes, that berated him without her needing to say a word.

"I'll be there tomorrow," she snapped, and he was sure that was the first time she had been angry with him, couldn't remember her ever barking at him like that before, baring her fangs.

The line went dead.

Maverick pulled the phone away from his ear and looked at it, and then at Rune. Rune slid him a look, one that clearly said the bigger male wanted to cuff him around the head for some reason.

"What's wrong with Winnie?" Rune looked from him to the phone.

Maverick shrugged. "I don't know. She wouldn't say. Just asked me to meet her."

He still didn't like that. It had him on edge, gearing up for a fight, and it was hard to shake off the urges building inside him, stopping them before they could seize control. He breathed through it as he texted her the address of the bar, as he stared at his phone, waiting for a response so he knew she had got it. His muscles tightened further with every second that trickled past, each of them feeling like an hour as he willed her to respond, part of him needing to know he could contact her whenever he wanted now.

A message came in. Three words.

I'll be there.

Was she angry with him? He didn't like the thought she might be. He didn't like the fact she had refused to tell him what was wrong either. There was something off about that, something he couldn't shake. He huffed and put it down to the decades he had spent at the compound, years that had moulded him into a male quick to doubt anyone and always looking for an ulterior motive, or a blade hidden in plain sight ready to plunge into his heart.

"I'm coming with you." Rune went to turn away from him and Maverick grabbed his arm, couldn't stop himself from pressing his fingers hard into it through his long-sleeve black T-shirt.

"No." Maverick looked across at him as he slipped his phone into the back pocket of his black jeans, met Rune's pale blue eyes and didn't let the look in them sway him. "I'm going alone."

"Mav," Rune started, and he could feel the lecture coming. "It's Winnie."

"I know. I know that… but I'd rather go alone. There's no need for both of us to go. You stay here with Callie." Maverick held his gaze, letting his friend see in his eyes the reason he couldn't let him come with him.

He trusted Bronwyn, but the bear in him was riled for some reason and he wasn't sure it was just restless because it knew someone he cared about was in danger. If he let Rune come with him and, gods forbid, something happened, he would never forgive himself. Rune was at the start of a new life, a better life, and Maverick didn't want anything to ruin that.

Maverick flicked a glance at Callie.

The black-haired wolf nodded slightly, her amber eyes silently telling him that she would keep Rune here and keep his mind occupied while Maverick was away from Black Ridge. Maverick hated it as much as Rune did whenever they were parted, always felt compelled to get back to his friend's side, a need that had been formed over the years they had spent together. It was a powerful bond, one that always pulled him back to Rune.

He and Rune both shared a similar bond with Bronwyn too. They had become like family in the few years that Winnie had been at the compound, and he needed to remember that. He needed to trust her. She wasn't a danger to him.

His bear side growled and groaned, swayed restlessly in a way that he realised had nothing to do with the feeling he was in danger, and had everything to do with the fact Winnie was.

Maverick stared out of the window at Black Ridge, not seeing the beauty or feeling the peacefulness of it as evening light bathed it. That restless feeling kept growing stronger, pounding inside him, driving him to do something.

He tensed, locking up tight when Rune placed a hand on his shoulder. His head whipped towards his friend.

"You good?" Rune's blue eyes searched his.

Maverick swallowed and nodded, ran a hand over his short black hair and exhaled hard. His brow furrowed as he looked at Rune, as the compulsion grew too strong to deny.

"Go. I'll make your apologies to the others. Callie won't mind, will you?" Rune looked at his mate.

She shook her head, her voice soft and warm. "I'll make sure they save you something to eat."

Maverick glanced at her, nodded his thanks, and stepped out of the door.

He peeled off his T-shirt and left it on the deck.

Heard Callie murmur to Rune.

"Tell me about Winnie. I figure she was at the compound too. What is it about her that has Maverick so worked up?"

Maverick burst into a dead run, putting Black Ridge behind him and heading for the glacier, the route he always took when he needed to work off some steam.

That question ringing in his mind.

CHAPTER 3

Bronwyn twisted the glass in front of her back and forth, watching the condensation form and the ice refuse to move. It remained almost still as she shifted the glass, floating serenely on top of the dark liquid. The bartender had given her a look when she had asked for a soda, and maybe she should have taken the silent prompt to order something stronger.

Her stomach had refused to settle from the moment she had heard Maverick's voice on the other end of the line, had given her hell during the long drive from Whistler. She had left immediately, hadn't returned to the pride to tell them where she was going, had just texted her aunt to let her know she had gone to stay with some friends for a few days and then got in her small car and started driving.

It had taken her all night to reach the remote town deep in the heart of the mountains and she was bone-deep tired, had downed several coffees at a local café and forced herself to eat something before she had plucked up the courage to go to the bar.

The Spirit Moose.

It resembled an ancient log lodge set in a large parking lot just outside the centre of town and the man who had been sweeping the deck that surrounded two sides of it had been surprised to see her when she had asked if it was open. When she had explained she was supposed to meet someone here, he had been sympathetic and had let her wait inside while he finished getting the bar ready for the day.

Around three hours ago, he had officially opened it up.

She glanced at her phone again, woke the screen and stared at the clock. She probably should have set a time to meet Maverick. Was it too late to text him?

Bronwyn rubbed sleep from her eyes, fighting off a yawn, and stared at the message he had sent her. He hadn't sounded happy about meeting her and she feared he knew she was up to no good, that he wouldn't come or that he had lured her here to see if she was setting him up for a fall. Her stomach somersaulted and she pressed her hand to it as she told herself that she was reading into things. She was nervous about seeing him, hated herself for doing this to him, and it was playing havoc with her.

Another minute ticked past.

Another minute without Maverick showing up.

Another minute without a call or message from the hunters who had her brother.

The sickness swelled again, made her tighten her grip on her stomach through her burgundy camisole, sure this time she would vomit. Every time she recalled how bleak her brother had looked, kneeling in that cell wearing only shorts, and how that male had looked hungry to hurt him, she wanted to be sick.

She'd had to stop several times during her long drive, pausing at the side of the road in the dark for some fresh air, gasping at it. Other times, she had dry heaved.

She cursed the hunters, acid scouring her veins, hatred darkening her heart. They had taken so much from her, and from Maverick and Rune, and now they wanted to take more.

Light burst across her eyes.

Bronwyn's gaze darted to the door, her eyes adjusting to the onslaught of sunshine, and she sagged as she saw it was just some human.

She went back to nursing her drink.

She had picked a table where she could see the door, one away from the bar to her right. That didn't stop people from looking at her. Several other tables had occupants now, locals and regulars judging by the way they talked, catching up with each other and the bartender, discussing the latest round of roadworks and some festival that was coming up. She listened to the air conditioning unit whirring, savouring how cool it kept the dark-walled room.

Her thoughts drifted again, straying to Maverick.

Bronwyn tensed when she felt eyes on her, flicked a glance at the male at the bar, one who was looking at her as he waited for his drink. Curiosity shone in his dark eyes as he adjusted his worn grey baseball cap and she hoped it was just because she was a new face in a small town and not born of any desire to try his luck with her.

"Thanks, Jon." The brunet male slid money across the bar and pushed away from it, coming to face her, his faded pale brown checked shirt falling open to reveal a grey T-shirt that hugged his slim frame. There were a few grease spots on the soft material and her sensitive nose said it was engine oil that had never quite washed out.

She willed him away from her. He might look her age at pushing thirty, but she was far too old for him and really not interested.

Apparently, he didn't get her silent message to leave her alone.

He strolled over to her, his heavy work boots making the wooden floor of the bar creak in places, and she tensed as he set his drink down on her table.

"What's a pretty girl like you doing drinking alone in the middle of the day?" he drawled.

Loomed over her.

Bronwyn fought the crush of her memories, told herself that he wasn't a threat to her and she wasn't back at the compound. He was just trying his luck and would leave her alone. He wouldn't try to make her do something she didn't want to do. He wouldn't.

But the way he towered over her had her fear rising despite her best efforts to tame it, had her bear side growing agitated, tearing her between running and lashing out at him. Both would be a bad choice. If she ran, she might miss Maverick. If she lashed out, she might accidentally kill the human.

"Waiting for someone." She forced the words out, put enough bite in them that he would hopefully get the message this time and leave her alone.

He dropped into the seat opposite her. She glared at his chest, couldn't bring herself to look him in the eye, and drew her drink closer to her as panic mounted, as those memories she tried to push out of her head flowed into it faster, a stream of them that had her dangerously close to lashing out to drive him away from her.

"Looks like you've been waiting a while." The man tapped one of the several empty glasses she had pushed to one side. "Doesn't look like this guy deserves your time."

It was quite the opposite.

Maverick deserved every second of her time and she would wait for him forever if she had to.

Plenty of shifters in the arena compound had thought they could do what they wanted with her from the moment she had arrived at a tender age of only seventy-six, two decades off maturing. She hadn't known much about the sort of things the males had wanted to do with her. Some of them had openly touted that they liked the fact she hadn't matured, that she was young and innocent, ripe for plucking.

She had feared they were going to carry out their threats, that she wouldn't be able to stop them.

And then Maverick had laid the largest of them out cold on the ground with a single blow.

She had thought he had wanted her to himself, had already heard about how violent he was and that he was one of the hunters' prized fighters.

So when he had grabbed her wrist and pulled her with him, she had been scared, and when he had pushed her into a cell where Rune had been waiting, she had been terrified.

Only he had grunted to Rune that she needed protecting, had told the fearsome black bear about what had happened to her, and something incredible had happened—she had suddenly found herself with two of the biggest, baddest bears as her bodyguards.

If it hadn't been for Maverick and Rune, she wouldn't have come out of the compound untouched and unscathed as she had. The two bears had taken care of her and most of the other shifter males had been sensible enough not to dare to try anything with her. The ones who had over the years had quickly learned that messing with her meant they were messing with Rune and Maverick.

"Come on, one drink." The male reached across the table for her hand.

Panic lanced her. "I—I'm sorry. Please leave me alone. I really am waiting for someone."

It didn't deter the human and panic turned to fear as he came closer to touching her.

A strong hand clamped down on his left shoulder and he grunted as he leaned in that direction, his face reddening as he tensed and grimaced.

"You deaf or just dumb?" The deep masculine voice that growled those words had her fear rapidly fading, flowing out of her as if a dam had burst. "The lady said to leave her alone."

The human was quick to make an exit when Maverick released him, left his drink behind in his haste to escape the grizzly who eased his six-six frame into the seat he had occupied.

Gods.

Bronwyn stared at him, unable to do anything else as her heart fluttered in her throat, as the sight of Maverick seared itself on her mind and lit her blood on fire. He was just as darkly handsome as she remembered, his clear grey eyes as sharp as a blade and his sculpted features making him look like he had just fallen out of Heaven. The only thing that was different about him was his black hair. No longer close-cropped, it was lush and thick, wild on top and long enough at the sides that she could run her fingers through it. The damp ribbons looked as if he had just stepped out of the shower, made her shiver as she imagined him naked and wet.

His grey eyes narrowed slightly, no trace of emotion in them, and then they lowered to take her in and a hint of surprise broke through the barrier he locked his feelings behind.

And Bronwyn swore there was a flicker of heat deep in the depths of his eyes.

She shivered inside at the feel of his gaze on her, a primal part of her awakening in response, filling her with an urge to tease him by pretending to neaten her pixie cut, maybe twirl one of the chestnut strands around her finger, tempting him into wanting to touch her.

And then he tossed a bucket of ice on the fire he had ignited.

"Little Winnie the Pooh." He shook his head, the corners of his mouth lifting slightly, stopping before they became a smile. "Was sure I'd never see you again."

She scowled at him and was tempted to pick him up on the fact she wasn't little anymore. She wasn't that girl he had taken care of in the compound. She had grown up, was mature now, her body awakening. Although, she had never felt fire the likes of which burned through her as Maverick gave her another slow once-over. Just a look from him had an inferno blazing in her blood, had her restless and unbolted the door on feelings she had never experienced before.

Like a wicked urge to growl and bare fangs at him, to provoke him.

Bronwyn shut down that urge.

Maverick leaned back in his chair and brought his arms up, locking his hands behind his head, causing his thick black fleece shirt to stretch tight around his biceps and forearms. Something was wrong. He might look relaxed to the casual observer, but she knew him better. He was on edge.

Her heart thundered for a different reason, racing as her mind screamed that she knew why he was on edge around her.

It was as she feared.

He knew she was up to no good.

He was expecting trouble, waiting for her to betray him. Gods, she couldn't do this. Just the thought of luring Maverick and Rune into a trap had her sick to her stomach again, made her want to rush to the ladies' room to vomit.

Maverick dropped his hands and sat up, the black slashes of his eyebrows knitting hard above intense grey eyes. "What's wrong, Winnie? What's this trouble you're in?"

Her hands shook as she toyed with her glass, as she debated spilling her guts and telling him everything, or maybe running for the door and not looking back. An image of Andrew with that male hunter looming over him, his blade poised to slit her brother's throat, flashed across her eyes and her fingers tensed against the glass.

It broke and she flinched as one of the pieces bit into her palm.

"Christ, Winnie." Maverick grabbed her hand, his eyes wide and wild as he pulled it to him. "Be more careful."

She could only stare at him as he grabbed one of the paper napkins from the dispenser and cleaned the blood from her palm, his expression growing tender as he dabbed at the shallow cut. He plucked another napkin, pressed it to her palm and held it there, applying gentle pressure to the wound.

His grey eyes lifted and locked with hers. "It's time you tell me what this is about."

She swallowed hard. Cursed herself. Hated herself. She had to do this though.

Maverick was strong. He could survive the cage. Her face crumpled, tears threatening to come at just the thought of him having to fight again. He would hate her for it. Never again would he look at her the way he was now, as if she meant something to him, was precious to him.

A thought crossed her mind. Maverick and Rune were strong. Strong enough to help her save her brother? She wasn't sure how many hunters were in the compound, wasn't sure if they were tracking her or somehow watching her. She wasn't sure of anything. No. She was sure of something.

If she asked Maverick to help her save her brother, he would do it. He wouldn't care how many hunters he had to go through. He wouldn't care that he might get himself killed. He would do it for her.

She had sworn she wouldn't tell Maverick and Rune what was happening, and she wouldn't, but she wasn't going to lie to him either. She was going to bend the truth a little.

"I saw some hunters in Whistler and I got spooked." She stared at her hand, at his strong fingers pressed against it, and focused on it, shutting everything else out. "My brother… he's gone missing. I know hunters have him."

"They might not." He stroked his fingers over hers, tensed and seemed to catch himself, and released her as he sat back. "Your brother in the habit of leaving you alone?"

She shrugged. "He visits Vancouver every month. Has been going for longer recently. Life at the pride isn't exciting enough for him."

Maverick rubbed the thin layer of stubble that coated his square jaw. "Hmm. Doesn't sound good."

"Will you come with me to see if we can find him?" She ached to ask him to come with her to help her save him, but she didn't know where she was supposed to take Maverick.

She glanced at her phone, hoping the hunters didn't call her right now, while she was with him. Maybe they were giving her time to make contact with Maverick and Rune. It was clear they didn't know where Maverick and Rune were, because they would have cut out the middleman and come to grab them instead.

Gods, what if that was their plan? What if they were tracking her via her phone or her laptop and were planning a raid? For all she knew, they could be using her as bait and had zero intention of releasing her brother.

She had been such an idiot.

"Come with me to Black Ridge. You'll be safe there, Winnie. Me and Rune will take care of you. It'll be like old times." Maverick's silver-grey eyes were cold again, the barrier back in place, concealing his emotions from her.

Did he really want things to be as they had been between them? With him acting like her big brother? She didn't want that. She wanted him to see her as she was now—a mature female who was on fire for him. She wanted to make him forget how things had been and want something different with her, something she felt would be fierce and powerful, as wicked as her dreams of him.

She considered pushing him to come with her, but she needed Rune too, knew in her heart that the hunters wouldn't be satisfied if she didn't bring both bears to them. Going with him would give her time to convince him and Rune to come with her, and would give the hunters time to call her with her next step.

Only it sounded as if Black Ridge was a place where more than only Maverick and Rune lived, brought to mind the big grizzly bear who had taken part in the raid that had freed them all, a bear who had given Maverick and Rune a place in his pride and had extended the same offer to her and her brother.

She didn't want to place even more people in danger.

"What if the hunters are tracking me? Maverick—" She dropped her gaze to the damp table and stared at his reflection in her spilled soda, unable to look him in the eye as fear got the better of her, as she struggled to tamp down the urge to tell him everything.

Maverick reached over the table and caught her hand, his look deadly serious as he growled.

"I'll protect you. If hunters come, I'll kill them all. I'll keep you safe. There isn't anyone in this world strong enough to take you from me, Bronwyn."

CHAPTER 4

Maverick was finding it hard to keep his eyes on the track as his black Ford F150 rumbled along it, every bump he hit jostling the female sitting next to him, making him even more aware of her than he already was.

If that was possible.

He couldn't stop looking at her, his gaze gravitating towards her despite his best efforts to keep it on the road so they didn't plummet into the bushes and trees that lined the drop to his right.

Bronwyn leaned against the open window there, her arm resting along the door and her head propped up on her hand. The sultry breeze that swept into the cab, carrying the scent of cedar and sunshine, tousled her short chestnut hair, brushing it from her face, and made the loose material on the lower half of her burgundy top flutter around her stomach and her jeans.

He did his best not to look at the top half of it, where it hugged her breasts, pressing them together to form cleavage.

She was right.

He flicked a glance at her when they hit a straight, lingered as the sunlight caught her face, revealing the light smattering of freckles across her cheeks and making her honey-coloured eyes shimmer with gold.

She wasn't a cub anymore.

She was all curves and temptation.

Had grown up far more beautiful than he had thought possible.

When he had stepped into The Spirit Moose and spotted her, he had been convinced he had to be imagining it was her, that he was mistaken and little Winnie hadn't shown up yet.

But then he had caught her scent.

Caught was an understatement.

It had hit him like a wrecking ball.

Like honey and cream, with a faint note of cinnamon. Delicious. Tempting. Had his mouth watering even now, and his mind racing along a dangerous track.

She had been silent since they had reached the road up to the trailhead, had taken to staring out of the window, and he had taken to staring at her. She had to be aware of how often he was looking at her. The thought that she might be had his gaze zipping back to the track and locking on it, because he had no right to gaze at her the way he was.

He glanced at her again.

Cleared his throat and tried to think of something to say.

"Sorry the radio is busted." Gods, did that sound as lame to her as it had to him?

She looked at him, those honey eyes tempting him into demanding she move a little closer to him. There was an ocean of space between them and he didn't like how she was pressed against the door, as if she wanted to be as far from him as she could get. Was he scaring her? She didn't have the best experience with males, had always been jittery whenever they got too close to her.

But she had never shied away from him.

"I like the sounds of the world. I don't think the birds have stopped singing for a second." She hit him with a dazzling smile and then stole it away from him, turning it on the valley instead. He had never been jealous of a valley before, but he wanted to growl as she beamed at it. "It's nice up here. The breeze is cooler and the view is beautiful, and I think I saw a mountain bluebird a while back."

"It's possible. We get a few of them breeding up here." He huffed as he had to slow the truck. "Got a few more annoying neighbours too."

The big male elk stopped to look right at him, as if it had understood him, and then proudly, and damned slowly, continued to cross the track. Bronwyn watched it with fascination in her bright eyes, tracking it until it had disappeared down the slope into the scrub.

Maverick pulled the truck away again and kept his focus on the road, just in case any other large ungulates wanted to jump out and wreck his vehicle and kill him and Winnie.

"You mentioned Whistler. Did you go back there after we escaped?" He wanted to glance at her but resisted.

She sighed. "Andrew wanted us to go back there, to our pride. We went straight there. Everyone was so pleased to see us."

Maverick remembered her brother. Not the strongest bear. The male had been easily swayed by the hunters, had done whatever they had wanted, even leaving his little sister undefended.

Bronwyn loved him though. Maverick recalled that clearly enough. She had always defended her brother, and for a small black bear, she had been quite ferocious at times. Rune had thought it was their bad influence. Maverick had figured it was just the depth of her love for her brother shining through.

He did glance at her now.

She had a little more spark these days, but she was still the same gentle female he had known back then. Twenty years hadn't changed that. He could see it in her eyes whenever she looked at him.

He pulled the truck up beside another one at the trailhead and put it into park. "We'll have to walk from here."

She was quick to slip from the cab and close the door. She raised her arms above her head and stretched, making her cleavage even more pronounced. Maverick pulled back on the reins before he growled at the sight of her and opened his door and dropped to the ground. He gave himself a moment, taking his time about shutting the door and locking up, needing it to regain control of himself.

Bronwyn seemed determined to wreck him, came around the back of the truck to his side and looked around her at the trees that enclosed the small parking area. "It really is beautiful up here."

Her eyes landed on him and he couldn't stop himself from staring at her. Stared so long that she grew awkward, fidgeted with the hem of her summer top and dropped her gaze there.

"Sorry. Just hard to believe it's really you. Twenty years… It's a long time." And it had changed her in ways he hadn't been prepared for.

He strode past her, needing some air that wasn't laced with her tempting scent, breathed deep of it as he wrestled his urges back under control.

She caught up with him, fell into step beside him as he slowed his pace, and her eyes darted around the forest.

"You really live up here?" She glanced at him but this time her gaze didn't linger. It leaped back to the trees.

"Sure do." He took in the forest too and the glimpses of mountains through the dense green canopy. The air was cooler in the shade of the towering pines, dropped a few degrees as they followed a trail down towards the creek. "Since we escaped."

"Who else lives here?" She lifted her head as they reached the creek, her eyes wide as she surveyed it. "This place makes Whistler look like a dump. It's gorgeous."

He frowned when she bent over right in front of him, giving him one hell of a view of her curvy ass as her jeans tightened over it. "What are you—"

She looked over her shoulder at him, still bent over, making the fire raging through his blood all the worse. "I was going to paddle."

Maverick grabbed her arm and pulled her upright. "You can paddle later. The creek runs through Black Ridge."

Was that his voice, so tight and scratchy? He cleared his throat, was quick to release her and distance himself. Maybe he should have let Rune come along. He rubbed the back of his neck, grimacing at how damp it was. Maybe he should have made Rune go to meet her by himself. Looking back, it would have been the better choice.

He started walking again, gulping down the air that wasn't laced with her scent, aware that any second now she would catch up with him. She managed it faster this time, walked beside him with a bounce in her step.

"So, are you going to answer my question?" she said and when he glanced at her, she added, "Who else lives here?"

"Saint and some others. Pride's been growing lately. Around nine of us living permanently at Black Ridge now."

"Nine?" Her eyes widened and her step slowed. "So many?"

He sensed the shift in her emotions, a trickle of fear that had him slowing too and turning towards her. "It'll be all right. You know Rune, and his mate is nice enough. And you remember Saint, right?"

"Saint," she echoed, her gaze distant, and then it sharpened. "He was the big grizzly who offered to let us join his pride too. I remember you wanted us to take him up on that offer."

Not just him, but she made it sound as if he had been the driving force behind trying to convince her to come live with them. Hell, maybe he had been. The thought of leaving her in the care of her brother hadn't sat well with him.

"I remember your brother growing a spine and refusing."

Her beautiful face darkened as he said that, fire flaring in her eyes, bringing out the gold. "Don't talk about Andrew like that."

He huffed, torn between apologising and walking away. Walking away won. He wrestled with himself as the distance between him and Winnie grew. What the hell was wrong with him today? He was normally abrasive, but it wasn't like him to be this caustic, not for a long time.

Not since the compound.

Maybe it was just her presence bringing that darker side of him to the fore so easily, memories of his time at the compound affecting his mood, agitating him and making him fall back into his old ways. Being an asshole had been the best way to keep himself safe at the compound, had kept everyone at a distance from him.

Except for Rune.

And Bronwyn.

He never had been able to bring himself to be like that with her, so what had changed? Why was he flipping so quickly between wanting to be nice to her and wanting to push her away that he was starting to get a headache?

Maverick massaged his temples, a need building inside him, one he would have to surrender to soon or he would only get worse. He was already looking for a fight. Soon, looking for one would turn into picking one, and he didn't want Winnie to be on the receiving end.

"Maverick?" Bronwyn's voice was small, cautious as she trailed a few feet behind him.

He sighed. "Sorry. Just… not in a good place mentally today. Didn't mean to be an asshole to you."

He wasn't going to apologise for being an asshole about her brother though. Andrew was a weak, spineless male who only really cared about himself. What she had told him was proof of that. Her brother was spending more and more time away from her, leaving her alone at her pride, at a time when she needed the support of her family.

She came up beside him again, glanced at him, and then her eyes came back to him and lingered.

Maverick tried to keep his focus on the hike, on the world around him, on anything but the curvy female beside him. Tried and failed. He was bone-deep aware of her, of how much she had changed in the years they had been apart.

When she had first arrived at the compound, she had been in her mid-seventies, had looked barely twenty in human terms, but in bear terms she had been an adolescent. He had felt protective of her then, had wanted to kill every male who had dared to come on to her or had thought they could do as they pleased with her.

She hadn't been mature, and gods, he hadn't wanted her to mature in that environment as he had been forced to. He hadn't wanted her to end up as messed up as he was, and he was messed up. He was deeply aware of that.

Just as he was deeply aware she had matured now.

For five years he had protected her, had taken better care of her than her own damned brother, had made sure she had come through the whole experience without ever being touched by a male or thrown into the cage to fight.

The one time their captors had tried to do that was a nightmare that still regularly haunted his sleep.

He had stepped up and told the hunters he would fight in her place.

Little Winnie hadn't wanted him to do it, had been distraught, but he hadn't given her a choice. Protecting her had taken priority over his own well-being, and he had taken a good beating in the cage that night, the hunters repaying him for his audacity in thinking he could make demands as he had.

It had been worth it though.

It had kept her safe.

And for once, he hadn't spent the fight eager to see if the hunters would reward him with a soft female to fuck in that cold, clinical holding room they always sent fighters to after a match.

He had been eager to get back to Winnie and see she was all right.

He gazed at her, couldn't keep his damned eyes off her.

Hell, she was all woman—all soft curves—and her scent was divine, driving him wild.

He moved closer to her as they passed through Cougar Creek, kept a wary eye on Rath and his brothers where they were lingering in the long sloping clearing that stretched a good two or three hundred feet up from the river.

"Are they shifters too?" Bronwyn's soft voice had his focus splitting between her and the cougars.

He grunted in response, didn't take his gaze off the males even though none of them were a threat to Winnie. When Rath's head swivelled towards him and Bronwyn, Maverick had to leash the urge to bare fangs at him, warning the dark-haired alpha away. Tension flooded him, had his muscles aching as he stared the cougar down, the need to fight rising swiftly now. Rath was a good fighter, could probably help Maverick ease this need growing out of control inside him, but the cost of surrendering to it would be high.

Saint had been working hard to smooth things over between their pride and the cougars, and starting a fight with them over nothing would only ruin everything his alpha had accomplished. He wouldn't be the one to wreck things, couldn't be. He needed Black Ridge. He needed his pride.

And he feared Saint would kick him out if he caused trouble with the cougars.

Bronwyn moved closer to him as they passed the clearing, as she gazed back at the cougars, wreaking havoc on his control. The urge to fight got twisted in his head, had hunger rolling through him as he grew painfully aware of how close she was to him, as her scent taunted him and lured his gaze to her.

He raked it over her curves, his mouth drying out as he took her in.

His cock stiffening in his jeans.

Gods, it was wrong of him to be attracted to her. She was like a little sister to him—or maybe she wasn't. As he gazed down at her, a feeling stirred inside him, one that whispered the truth to him.

Their relationship had never been brother-sister.

He had always been fiercely protective of her.

And looking back, he didn't feel it was because she had been like a sister to him. He had the feeling that maturing in captivity, in that depraved and dark world, had made it impossible for him to recognise what she was back then, or maybe he had always known she was meant for him and he just hadn't wanted to acknowledge it.

Because he wasn't worthy of her.

Maverick felt that keenly in his soul as he looked at her.

Bronwyn was like a light that shone too brightly—it hurt to look at her.

He swallowed hard as she glanced at him, his brow furrowing slightly as he tried to think of something to say, as her soft look tied his tongue into a knot and had him feeling unsteady.

A little frown creased her brow as her eyes softened further.

She canted her head slightly. Blinked. Opened her mouth and looked as if she wanted to say something.

His lips parted and he wrestled with himself, tried to line up the words to tell her that he was glad to see her, to tell her that she had changed everything for him when she had arrived at the compound, that she had been a blessing in disguise for him.

That he should have recognised back then what she was to him.

That she was meant for him.

That he wasn't good enough for her.

"Pooh Bear!" Rune's deep voice startled him, had his shoulders tensing and his head whipping around to face the direction of Black Ridge.

Rune strode along the pebbly bank of the creek, his pace swift, his blue eyes bright with warmth as he grinned from ear to ear and opened his arms to Bronwyn. She was quick to run to him, to burrow into his arms as he wrapped them around her, hugging her tightly.

Making Maverick want to growl.

Making him wish he had done that, but at the same time feel glad that he hadn't. Being close to her had been wreaking havoc on him as it was and he was deeply aware of the reason why now, his eyes wide open at last.

It didn't change anything though.

It couldn't.

CHAPTER 5

Rune placed his arm around Bronwyn and led her towards Black Ridge. What Rune was saying as he angled his head towards her was lost on Maverick as he stared at her. She turned her cheek to him as she smiled and laughed at whatever Rune had told her.

An ache built inside Maverick.

Not a need to fight or run this time.

He ached for her to look at him like that—for her to laugh and smile with him like that.

She had been on edge since he had walked into the bar, had been tense around him for some reason, maybe even a little withdrawn, giving him the impression she wanted to keep her distance from him.

But she was a completely different person with Rune.

And gods, it hurt.

He tipped his head back and stared at the clear blue sky, breathed deep of the cool air and exhaled hard. What the hell was he doing? He closed his eyes. No good would come of this. He shouldn't have brought her here. He should have told her to go back to her pride. He should have put as much distance between them as possible.

Her gaze landed on him.

Maverick heaved another long sigh and followed her and Rune, trailing after them, lost in the war happening in his head and his heart, a war the sensible part of him needed to win.

He and Winnie didn't belong together.

Fate had been cruel to make him her fated one.

She deserved someone better.

"Here, come and meet Callie." Rune's voice cut into his thoughts and Maverick realised they had reached the clearing in the heart of Black Ridge.

And everyone was waiting in it, loitering around the unlit firepit that was close to Saint's cabin.

Bronwyn tensed, an almost imperceptible tightening of her shoulders that most would have missed, but not him. He was too deeply attuned to her to miss even the slightest change in her mood.

"No one here is going to hurt you, Winnie," Rune said, almost a growl, and Maverick was glad his friend had noticed the spike in her nerves.

Callie was quick to come forwards, leaving the twin blond bears, Knox and Lowe, with their human mates.

Saint remained sitting on the step of the raised deck of his cabin with Holly tucked close to him, his dark eyes watching Bronwyn closely. His alpha must have been fooling around with his cougar mate in the creek that ran to the right of his cabin, because he was wearing khaki shorts and a faded black T-shirt, and his brown hair was damp. His petite black-haired female was dressed in similar clothing, her shorts made from cut-off jeans and her top a purple tank. Around her bare feet, the boards of the steps were damp.

Callie's amber eyes were bright as she greeted Bronwyn.

Maverick kept tabs on Bronwyn as the others came forwards, keeping his distance from them all. Knox and Lowe were polite enough, their blue eyes warm as they welcomed her to Black Ridge.

Skye nudged her mate, Knox, out of the way, a mischievous glint to her dark eyes as she reached out and feathered her fingers through Bronwyn's hair. "I'd love a cut like this. Knox likes my braids though."

She ran her hand down one of her twin braids.

Knox's low growl and the heat that shone in his eyes said the reason for him liking her braids was sexual, and Maverick really didn't need that mental image of the big bear holding on to them as he took his mate.

Flashes of females spread before him like that shot through his mind, a replay of every one he had taken while they were on their knees.

He needed a run.

His body felt too tight.

He stared beyond Saint's cabin, towards the mountains and the glacier there, his heart pounding faster, the need to run growing stronger as Bronwyn's scent hit him again and he felt her eyes on him.

Maverick took a hard step forwards.

"And this is Saint. You probably don't remember him."

Those words leaving Rune's lips and the hint of fear that laced Bronwyn's scent snapped Maverick back to her, purging the need to run and replacing it with a need to remain, to move closer to her and ensure his alpha didn't frighten her.

"I remember you." Bronwyn bravely stepped forwards as Saint pushed to his feet.

Saint took the steps down from his cabin and closed the distance between them. The big alpha towered a good foot taller than her, made her look small and triggered a need in Maverick, a powerful urge to close ranks with her.

That need only intensified as Saint's dark eyes narrowed, his jaw setting beneath his beard.

"You're our guest here, but we have rules. You cause any trouble at Black Ridge and you deal with me." Saint held her gaze, his features set in hard lines as he laid down the law.

"Dial it back," Maverick growled. "Winnie the Pooh is a good girl."

Her shoulders tensed and she glared over them at him, and he could see in her honey-coloured eyes that his words had hit a nerve. Good. He needed some distance between them, needed her to see that he was no good for her. She would be better off with any other male in this world.

Just the thought of her with someone else made him want to roar.

Made him want to rage.

To fight.

Bronwyn turned on him, her eyes flashing dangerously. "I told you not to call me that! I'm not a cub now. I'm not little Winnie the Pooh, or Pooh

Bear, or any other damned pet name you had for me when I was a girl. I'm not that little girl anymore, Maverick."

He was aware of that.

Too damned aware.

Rune cracked a rare grin. "You certainly aren't. You're all grown up now. Isn't she, Mav?"

Callie growled at him. Maverick was tempted to do the same.

He grunted, but refused to commit to an answer. The last thing he needed was Winnie growing aware of the fact that the moment he had set eyes on her again, he had noticed she was all grown up. Hell, it was hard not to notice how curvy she was now, how she had filled out in all the right places, and how beautiful she was. It was driving him mad.

Pushing him dangerously close to the edge.

He clung to that fragile distance between them, holding on to it as if it were a life raft, his only hope of surviving this unscathed.

He glanced towards the glacier again.

Needed to run.

"You can bunk in one of the cabins across the creek. Rune set one up in case I brought you back here." Maverick refused to look at her, kept his gaze on the glacier, that need pounding inside him, drumming harder and faster, pushing him to obey it. Maybe he could hit the lodge and stay there until Rune had dealt with Winnie's problem and she was gone. It was tempting. "Rune can show—"

"You'll have to do it." Rune cut him off and Maverick glanced at him, barely bit back a growl as Callie pulled Rune towards their cabin at the far end of the clearing, beyond the wooden bathroom-come-storage building that stood in the centre of all the cabins.

Rune tripped along behind his mate as she growled and snarled, an air about her that said Rune's remark about Bronwyn had triggered a need to stake a claim on him.

Great.

Maverick flexed his fingers, struggling now. His skin felt as if it was tightening around his muscles, choking him, and he wanted to claw it all off, ended up loosening a few buttons on his black shirt as he felt as if he couldn't breathe. He needed to run. He was all too aware of what would happen if he didn't burn off some energy. He would want to fight. With Rune occupied, he would have no way to vent himself, would grow aggressive towards everyone, trying to make a fight happen.

"Come back in an hour and we'll have dinner on the go. I thought we could grill up some steaks and you could get to know everyone a little better." Lowe's blue eyes lit up as he rolled up the sleeves of his light green checked shirt. "Like a welcome party."

Bronwyn's gaze seared Maverick, something crossing her eyes that he couldn't interpret. "I'm feeling a little tired from my journey. I drove through the night. Maybe I should just turn in early."

"We'll postpone the party until tomorrow then." Lowe's smile was understanding.

Far too fucking gentle and sweet.

Maverick battled the black urge that surged through him.

One that only grew worse when Bronwyn smiled back at Lowe and nodded. Maverick wanted to punch the male, the seething, wretched part of him that was looking for a fight labelling Lowe as the perfect candidate to be on the receiving end of his aggression.

Maverick grabbed Winnie's arm and marched her around Saint's cabin on the creek side of it, away from all the other males. He kept his gaze locked on the small cabin on the other side of the rippling river, refused to look in the direction of his one that stood near one of the bends, close to Saint's cabin. If he looked at it, he would want to take her there.

Letting her set foot in his cabin would be a mistake.

Being alone with her right now would be a mistake.

He needed to run.

"Which is your cabin?" Her soft voice invaded his thoughts, slicing through them, separating one urge from another for once. Fighting lost out to his other primal need, one he wouldn't be indulging with her.

He grunted and pointed to it, wanted to tell her to stay the hell away from it for her own sake, but ended up saying different words.

"I'm just there if you need anything." And by anything, he meant anything.

He clenched his jaw. No, he didn't. He mentally drew a line between them, shoved the urges she awakened in him into a box and locked it. It wasn't going to happen.

He released her and picked his way across the boulders that acted as steppingstones across the creek, not bothering to check whether she was following him. He didn't need to. He was hyper-aware of her as she made her way from one boulder to another, muttering to herself about how she didn't have long legs and was worried she would fall into the water.

Maverick denied the urge to turn around and help her. If she fell into the creek, she would get a little wet, that was all. It wouldn't kill her. The water was only a couple of feet deep.

He stomped up the steps onto the raised deck of the nearest cabin, one that stood on the pebbly bank just forty feet back from the river. It faced his cabin, had a nice view of the other side of Black Ridge and the mountains, and it had been recently renovated. She would be comfortable here.

Far away from him.

She finally reached him, a little out of breath as she clutched her bag in a death grip. Her smile was bright as she took the steps up to him.

"I thought I was going to fall in there for a moment. Would have been one way to get a new laptop." She released her bag and peered past him, into the window on the door of the cabin. "This looks nice. Cosy."

She turned her back to the cabin and sighed.

"What a view."

He had just been thinking the same thing as he had gazed at her.

Maverick shoved the door open and stomped inside, torching that thought. He really needed to run.

He kept his distance from her as he checked the cupboards of the small kitchen next to the door in the open-plan room. "Rune set you up with plenty of snacks and stuff. Water. Tea and coffee."

The damned black bear had thought of everything apparently. There were even feminine products on the counter near the sink—deodorant and a razor, one of the nice bottles of soap from the larder. Maverick kept his eyes off the last one, not needing to feed his already busy imagination more fuel. He was not going to imagine Winnie all naked and in the bath, soaping herself up.

He flexed his fingers again. Shook them, wishing he could shake off the tension just as easily.

"You can boil the kettle on the stove. Bathroom is in the building in the middle of the other cabins back there. Should be a flashlight in one of the drawers if you need to go out at night." He gave the small room an awkward once-over, unsure what else to do. "I'll, uh… I'll leave you to it."

She moved a few steps into the room, towards the log burner, and he edged past her.

Froze when she touched his arm.

Maverick looked at her.

Her smile hit him hard, flooded him with a need to tug her to him and hold her when it wobbled, betraying her nerves. "Thank you."

Maverick shrugged it off.

Her hand trailed off his arm as he backed towards the door.

He hated the way she looked at him as if he was her saviour.

When he was a monster.

CHAPTER 6

Bronwyn was dreaming. The same dream she'd had a thousand times. She moaned and arched to meet the powerful hard body of the male on top of her, dug her fingers into his shoulder as he moved inside her. She clung to him as she breathed hard, as he panted against her neck between kisses, laved her with his tongue and tightened his grip on her thigh.

On a low wicked growl, he shifted his hand to her backside and held it in a fierce, bruising grip, and thrust faster, deeper, ripping a groan from her lips as he dominated her. She sank against the hard surface beneath her that chilled her bare back, shuddered and ached for more as he pulled her closer to him, holding her hips up as they hit thin air. He grunted as he curled his hips, as he plunged deeper still, every frantic thrust making her breath hitch as she soared higher.

His free hand came down on her shoulder, pinned her to the table as he moved faster still, his breath fanning her neck, teasing her nape as it swirled around her. She wrapped her legs around his waist, worked her body against his, seeking that one push she needed to tip her over the edge. She tensed around him, clenching and unclenching, desperate now as his sweat-slicked body stuck to hers, as he drove into her and his fingers dug into her flesh, adding a spark of pain to the pleasure rolling through her.

Her entire body was on fire, blood burning as she strained.

A cry burst from her lips as release hit her in a blinding rush, as her body jacked up off the table and every inch of her quivered.

His grip on her tightened as he plunged deep into her, as he arched backwards and roared as he came, spilling inside her.

She drowsily stared at his face as bliss swept through her, each throb of his length causing an aftershock of pleasure to ripple along her nerves.

His grey eyes opened and locked with hers.

Bronwyn shot up in bed, panting hard and tingling all over, struggling to catch her breath as her heart thundered. She pressed her hand to her bare chest and sank onto the damp mattress on an exhale, stared at the ceiling as she slowly relaxed.

It was always the same.

It was always Maverick.

Her breaths evened out, her pulse settling as she drifted in the warm haze, the aftermath of her dream of him. This one had been particularly intense. Because she had seen him again? It had felt more real this time. She drew down a deep breath and caught his lingering scent in the cabin, moaned as her skin felt too tight, as need rolled through her again in response to the earthy masculine smell of cedar with a hint of smoke.

She focused on the world outside the cabin, trying to sense if anyone was nearby, and then bit her lip and skimmed her fingers down her collarbone. Her pulse jacked up again as she closed her eyes and lost herself in a fantasy, imagining it was Maverick's tongue stroking her as she swept her fingers around the curve of her breast and teased her nipple. Her other hand glided down her stomach, beneath the covers, and she moaned as she touched herself, as she rocked into it and gave herself over to need. It took only a few brushes of her fingers to have her coming undone again, her hips lifting off the mattress as release rolled through her.

Bronwyn sagged into the mattress, hoping she was sated this time, that she could see Maverick without making a fool of herself. She grimaced as she remembered what he had told her about the bathroom and what she had noticed during her exploration of the cabin yesterday. She was going to have to wash up in the sink before she saw anyone. The last thing she needed was Rune or Maverick smelling it on her.

Oh gods, she would die of embarrassment.

She looked over at the nightstand to her left, one of a pair in the loft bedroom, and rolled towards it. She grabbed her phone and switched it on. The signal was poor. No messages or missed calls though.

A knot formed in her stomach again as she stared at the screen. What was she doing? Could she really lure Maverick and Rune into a trap after everything they had done for her? She wasn't sure that she could. She didn't want to hurt them, but then she didn't want to hurt her brother either.

She sat up and pushed the covers aside, slipped from the bed and grabbed her clothes. Her senses stretched around her again. She was still alone. She hurried naked down the stairs to the ground floor of the cabin and set her clothes down on the small counter near the sink.

Made fast work of washing herself using the water and soap, and then drying herself with a towel.

Mostly because the damned door didn't have a lock.

She wasn't sure what would be worse—Rune or Maverick smelling what she had done alone in this cabin in her bed or one of them walking in on her while she was naked and desperately trying to wash the evidence away.

Her cheeks heated at the thought of either of those things happening.

Really heated when she thought about Maverick walking in on her while she was nude.

Her mind raced forwards, her overactive hormones quick to leap on that thought to have several scenarios playing out in her head, all of them wicked. She growled and shut them down, dressed quickly in her jeans and burgundy camisole top in the hope it would stop her newly-awakened needs from hijacking control again. Someone should have warned her that maturing sucked.

Although, her body hadn't been this out of control back in Whistler.

Back at her pride, plenty of males had noticed her maturing, and some of them had even offered to help her out with taming her new urges and needs. None of them had appealed to her though. Her mind had been firmly set on one male, her body awakening for only him, and he had been nothing but a dream until now.

It hit her that was the reason she was constantly battling a primal hunger that felt as if it was going to seize control at any moment and make her do something embarrassing.

Like climbing Maverick like he was a tree in front of everyone.

Maverick was the problem.

She had been fantasising about him, feeding the primal beast inside her with dreams of him, both while she had been asleep and while she had been awake and alone in her bed.

In the shower.

In the woods even.

Her cheeks flamed as she recalled that one.

She had been on a hike and had found a quiet spot near a waterfall, and had pictured Maverick under the spray, Maverick striding towards her through the clear water, running his hands over his head to slick his wet black hair back, water rolling down his bare body.

Maverick grabbing her and pulling her against him.

Bronwyn shrieked as a knock sounded, tensed and whirled towards the door, her heart jammed into her throat.

"Sorry!" Rune hollered.

Her legs shook as she hurried to the door, as she paused with her hand on the knob and breathed slowly to settle her racing pulse, and tame her unruly desire. When she had both back under control, she opened the door and plastered a smile on her face.

Rune ran a hand around the back of his neck, scrubbed his close-cropped dark hair, and lifted a tray he held balanced on his other hand. "Thought you might like some fresh coffee. Didn't mean to startle you."

She stepped back to let him in, shut the door behind him and pulled the blind up, her hands trembling a little as she realised how close she had been to Rune showing up while she was undressed. Gods, she was glad she had drawn the drapes and put the blind down last night before hitting the sack. Rune might have gotten an eyeful while he had been crossing the creek.

"Coffee smells good," she said, fighting a grimace.

Rune set the wooden tray down on the kitchen counter and frowned over his shoulder at the log burner. "Not got that going yet?"

"I only just woke up." She went to move to the burner.

Rune beat her to it, strolled over to it and eased down, his black jeans tightening over his thighs and his T-shirt stretching taut across his broad back as he worked to build her a fire. "Gets chilly in the mornings even in summer this high up."

She rubbed her arms, deeply aware of that as her skin turned to gooseflesh.

Rune glanced at her, his blue eyes holding a hint of concern, a look that transported her back to the compound. He had always looked at her like that, had always been worried about her. For a male who many had viewed as a violent brute, a dangerous and often unhinged bear, he had a big soft heart hidden beneath his hard exterior.

A heart she felt sure had been stolen by the pretty wolf she had met.

"*So…* Callie is your mate?" She poured coffee into two mugs, leaving the third empty. She stared at that one, sure Rune had brought it for Maverick.

Was he expecting Maverick to join them? Her heart drummed against her ribs at the thought of seeing him again after her dream of him.

"She sure is. Only been mated a few weeks, so we're still in that honeymoon stage. She's looking forward to getting to know you better later. If you want, I can ask her to drop in, maybe bring you some warmer clothing?" Rune shut the door of the burner and pushed to his feet.

She rubbed her arm again. "Noticed my astounding lack of sensible clothing, huh?"

Rune's lips curled into a faint smile. "Always noticed everything about you, Winnie. Never was anything you could hide from me. Guess that's why Maverick always used to tease me about being your adoptive father."

She smiled at him, warming inside as she thought about how things had been between them. Maverick was right about Rune. He had always been more than brotherly towards her. He had been fatherly. She had the feeling he had played the father role for Maverick too, back when he had arrived at the compound, before he had matured.

Now they were like brothers.

Were closer than she was with her own flesh and blood.

She stared at the coffees and rubbed her arm as she thought about Andrew, as sorrow laced with hurt swept through her, drawn up by how things between them had changed over the years despite her attempts to keep things as they had been. She had been close to him once, a long time ago now, before the compound, and part of her longed to be that close to him again, to heal the distance between them.

A distance she didn't understand.

Some part of her was convinced she had done something wrong, had been a bad sister somehow, but whenever she took a moment to be alone with her thoughts, she couldn't think of anything she had done to drive him away.

She pushed aside her sombre thoughts, trying to rid herself of them, but it was impossible as she felt Rune's gaze shift to her, as she thought about Maverick, and the choice she had to make.

Sorrow over how things had changed between her and Andrew morphed into sorrow over the fact she was considering betraying two bears who had been nothing but good to her.

When the air in the room thickened, the sense that Rune was waiting for her to say something pressing down on her, she forced herself to speak.

"I left in a hurry. I thought I had a fleece or a jacket in the back of my car, but apparently not. I must have taken it out to clean it." She poured milk into her coffee and sighed as she stared at the empty mug. "You want milk or cream in yours?"

"I'll take it black." Rune reached around her and swiped the mug before she could pass it to him. "Maverick didn't say much about the trouble you're in. He headed off for a run shortly after getting you settled."

She frowned at him, pausing with her mug near her lips. "He didn't come back from that run? Should we be out looking for him?"

Her hands shook as fear swept through her, thoughts that the hunters might have tailed her to Black Ridge and already captured Maverick filling her with a desperate need to forget everything and search for him, even when she didn't know the valley.

Rune waved her away. "Nah. He's fine. Probably won't see him until the afternoon. When he gets like this—"

She didn't like the way he cut himself off or the look he gave her, one that spoke volumes. He thought he had said too much and was holding things back from her.

"Like what?" She took a step towards him, lifted her hand and gripped his bare arm. "Like what, Rune?"

He looked as if he didn't want to tell her and that only made her want to press him harder, filled her with a need to know what was wrong with Maverick, increasing her need to find him and make sure he was safe.

Rune heaved a sigh.

Turned away from her and gazed out of the window in the door.

"Maverick… he never adjusted well. He… Sometimes he needs space. Sometimes running is enough. Sometimes he goes to the lodge for a week… or a month. It's his way of coping." He glanced at her and away again, his ice-blue eyes narrowing into a hard look that had a hint of regret, or possibly shame, about it. He sipped his coffee, lowered his mug and heaved another long sigh. "Sometimes it isn't space he needs. Sometimes we both need to fight. Maverick especially. Fighting… It's all he's really known."

Bronwyn pressed a hand to her stomach as it churned, as her heart raced and she struggled for air. She had never felt so wretched. So evil. Maverick and Rune were still trying to overcome their past and here she was planning to plunge them back into that hell.

"I thought you'd… I thought things would be better now… for both of you." She set her mug down, no longer in the mood for coffee.

"This isn't something we can just put behind us, Winnie." Rune opened the door and stepped towards it, breathed deep as cold air rushed into the room. His eyes closed and his features slackened, and she ached as she looked at him and realised he needed to feel the air on his face, on his skin, because he needed to remind himself he was free of that wretched place. "I'm coping better than Mav… I think. He matured in that compound… in that arena. Fighting is all he really knows. It's how he copes with everything. Life has been difficult for him since we left that place."

He turned towards her, his eyes opening and locking on hers, the look in them stilling her right down to her breathing.

"If you're here to act on the feelings you have for Maverick—"

"Feelings?" she blurted, tried to line up a denial and faltered.

"I told you, Winnie. I noticed everything about you. I'm not blind. Maverick might be, but I'm not. I always saw the way you looked at him. He's been through a lot—"

"I know that!" she snapped, her pulse thundering as nerves rushed through her, colliding with fear and shock, and disgust at herself. She wanted to scream at him to stop talking about how much they had been through, wanted to break down and confess the real reason she was here. She wanted to tell him that she would never hurt Maverick, but how could she when she was here to do just that? Instead of everything she wanted to say, she put something out there that she had held locked inside her for as long as she could remember. "You're right. I have a crush on Maverick. I think I've had it since the moment I met him. You can't tell him. Please, Rune? It's not the reason I'm here. I swear. I know he doesn't feel the same way. I'm not even on his radar. I'm just a little sister to him."

And gods, it hurt to think that, to put it out there and realise it was the truth.

She was always going to be little freckled-face Winnie the Pooh to Maverick.

Rune placed his mug down next to hers. "How long ago did you mature? Two… maybe three years?"

"Three," she muttered, her heart too heavy for her to put any strength into her voice as she thought about Maverick, as she realised he was never going to look at her in the way she wanted.

"I'll keep your secret, but in return I want to know something. Is it still a crush or did it become something more when you matured?"

She jerked her head up, her gaze colliding with his. "What do you mean by that?"

Rune stepped towards the door, stopped at the start of the deck, and stared at the world.

"Take a good hard look at your feelings before Maverick comes back and you see him again, and ask yourself something."

He looked back at her.

"What does it feel like when you find your fated mate?"

CHAPTER 7

Bronwyn wasn't sure how long she had been sitting on the top step of the deck, staring at the river and the cabins on the other side—not seeing them. Her gaze was turned inwards; her mind fixated on mulling over what Rune had said and the reason she was here.

She couldn't do this.

Even when she knew she had to.

Failure wasn't really an option.

She had to hurt one person she loved or the other.

But how was she supposed to decide between them?

Movement far off to her right caught her attention and her gaze shifted there, locking on the male striding along the pebbly shore on the other side of the creek. Sunlight shimmered across his damp bare chest, the powerful muscles of his arms tensing as he flexed his fingers around the shirt he gripped in his left hand. He didn't seem to notice her, but gods, she noticed him.

She wanted to growl at the sight of Maverick, wanted to stake a claim on him and drive every female in the vicinity away from him, even the mated ones.

Could Maverick be her one true mate?

His grey eyes remained firmly locked on his cabin as his long black jean-clad legs chewed up the distance between him and it, but as soon as he was in line with her, his head swivelled towards her.

Her entire body seemed to sing in response to him looking at her, had her heart fluttering in her throat as his gaze seared her and her blood heating to boiling point.

Maverick shifted course, not slowing his pace as he strode towards her, every muscle on his torso shifting in a symphony that had her body singing his praises. She had seen him shirtless before, but it had never hit her like this, triggering urges that were strong and startling, came dangerously close to wrenching control from her.

Water surged around his legs as he waded into the creek, not bothering with the steppingstones, making him look like something out of one of her fantasies as he prowled towards her, looking wild and wickedly alluring.

Only he was very real.

She was deeply aware of that as he stopped in the middle of the river, knee-deep in water, and bent over, dunked his shirt into the creek and used it to wash himself off.

Her mouth dried out.

Bronwyn stared hard as he ran the damp shirt over his body, the water glistening as it caught the sunlight, the sight of glittering droplets clinging to his honed muscles sending her temperature soaring. When he bent and scooped water over his head, straightened and ran his free hand over the tousled black lengths of his hair as rivulets trickled over the sculpted planes of his face, she was done for.

Her dreams were going to be seriously different from this point forward, would always start with this moment as it seared itself on her mind.

Maverick waded towards her, picked up pace again as he reached the shore, his clear grey eyes intense as he locked them on her again.

A shiver rolled through her.

If she hadn't already been in love with him, she might have fallen for him in this moment. Heck, she thought she might have fallen in love with him all over again her heart was beating so fast, her palms damp and nerves rising as he closed the distance between them.

He ran a hand over his hair again, squeezing more water from it. She followed a rivulet that ran down his neck and over his collarbone, and then darted down the broad slabs of his pectorals.

"You settle in all right?" His deep voice rolled over her, swept her away and had her gaze leaping back up to meet his.

She forced a nod. If he was expecting her to be able to make small talk while he was standing half-naked before her, he was going to find out very quickly that she was incapable of speaking right now. The sight of him was addling her mind, had her gaze constantly dropping to take in his glorious bare torso. She wanted to growl at just the sight of him, was battling a fierce need to stand and bare fangs as some deep primal instinct roared at her to dominate him.

To push him into reacting.

Heat rolled through her as she mulled over what Rune had said to her again and studied how she felt as Maverick towered before her, so temptingly close to her.

"Got everything you need?" He slung his wet shirt over his shoulder and held it there, his biceps tensing and his corded forearm flexing as he gripped it.

She nodded again.

Was sorely tempted to shake her head and tell him she didn't have everything she needed.

Because she didn't have him.

And gods, she needed him.

"Not very talkative today. Thoughts got your tongue all tied up?" He eased another step closer, concern emerging in his eyes as he ran them over her.

"No." She pushed that word out. "Yes. A little."

Not a lie. She was thinking about him, about the wicked urges he ignited in her, and it had her speechless.

The corners of his lips tilted upwards.

When he looked as if he might leave, she panicked and went from not being able to talk to not being able to shut up in the blink of an eye.

"Rune dropped by. He brought me coffee, which I badly needed, and said his mate might have something I could wear when the air is chilly." She picked at her jeans and tried not to lower her gaze to his chest, but her eyes betrayed her, swiftly took in the broad slabs of his pectorals and the way his abs flexed with each breath before leaping back up to meet his. "He mentioned you'd gone running."

Maverick almost smiled. "Yeah. I had too much energy. Needed to work some off. I wanted to drop in on Misty too."

Bronwyn growled.

It came out of nowhere.

Startled her.

And Maverick too judging by the way his grey eyes widened slightly.

Because she had threatened him.

Because he had mentioned a decidedly feminine name and the look in his eyes had been warm, affectionate, and her bear side had immediately grown restless, thoughts that he might have a female triggering a need to fight that went beyond a primal need to dominate him. She wanted to fight him, to make him submit to her and admit that he belonged to her.

"Misty is a black bear." Maverick said each word slowly, as if he was choosing his words carefully, or maybe he was just feeling her out, studying how she responded to that.

"Like me?" She was a black bear.

Maverick was a grizzly.

Not that it mattered.

Her fated mate could be anything from a human to a fallen angel.

"Not like you." Maverick came and leaned against the post of the railing beside her, a smile in his eyes but not on his lips. "Misty and Brook are the animal sort. They're sisters that Rune took in as cubs, raised them when their mother was callously shot by hunters while sleeping in their winter den."

"That's terrible." Her brow furrowed, her heart going out to the twin bears as the raging need to dominate Maverick swiftly faded, a calm replacing it as her bear side settled, satisfied that Maverick hadn't been with another female. "Hunters suck. All kinds of them. Just like Rune to take on being their father though."

"He does make a good dad." Maverick finally smiled, his whole face lighting up with it, and her heart skipped a beat as it hit her and had desire pulsing in powerful waves through her. "Always taking cubs under his wing."

She smiled too, but it wobbled as nerves got the better of her, as she looked into Maverick's eyes and wondered what he had made of her outburst. She had threatened him, over a female, something she had never done before. Could she blame her overactive hormones? She was still riding out the effects of maturing, finding her balance. It seemed like a reasonable excuse to her.

Maverick twisted and planted his back against the post, so close to her that her arm would brush his hand if she leaned a little to her left. He crossed his feet at his ankles and sighed as he stared across the river, towards the five cabins situated there.

His scent swirled around her, rich and earthy, cedar laced with a faint undernote of smoke. Her gaze drifted to him again, drawn to him against her will, and she gazed up at him, heat blooming in her veins as her senses locked onto him. The temptation to lean towards him and close the distance between them down to nothing was tremendous, almost hijacked control of her. Fear of what might happen held her back.

What if she made a move and he rejected her? What if she brushed his skin with hers and he only looked horrified? Nerves were swift to rise inside her as she lowered her gaze to his arm, as she battled to find the courage to do something and fought to hold herself back at the same time. She stood on a precipice, afraid of what might happen if she tried to turn their friendship into something more. She didn't want to ruin things between them.

She looked up at his face, her eyes tracing his profile, putting every sculpted plane to memory all over again.

When they reached the strong line of his jaw, she couldn't help but notice the tiny number and letter inked on the back of his neck.

223-B.

A number given to him when he had been captured and had entered the hunter compound.

She swallowed hard at the reminder of what he had been through, lifted her hand and placed it over her own number as guilt churned inside her again, the peace she had been feeling shattering as reality came flooding back in.

She wasn't here as his friend, or to see if they could be something more.

She was here to hurt him. To betray him.

Her gaze dropped to her knees as shame rolled over her, as a desperate need to confess everything surged through her, battering her resolve, pulling her between admitting the reason she was here and keeping silent to protect her brother.

Maverick's gaze landed on her. Seared her. Worsened the ache in her chest and her stomach as it lingered.

"It's nice he has Callie now." Those words were quiet as they left his lips, a distant edge to them that had her wanting to ask what he was thinking and gave her the impression his mind was traversing the same route as hers had been.

What it would be like to have a mate of her own.

But there was something else she sensed in him that had her asking a different question, a tension that had an obvious cause, at least to her.

"He's not going to just forget about you, Maverick. Having a mate doesn't change someone that much. You're his best friend."

He huffed and cast a look at her. "That obvious, huh?"

To her it was.

She nodded and gave a small shrug. "I'd be feeling the same way if my brother found his mate… or maybe I feel that way already. He spends so much time in Vancouver these days."

Maverick's gaze lingered on her face as she looked across the creek, her chest hurting as she thought about her brother.

"You should have come to live here instead. Been worried about you for twenty years, thinking I'll never see you again, and now here you are." He planted his hand on the top of her head as she looked up at him, warmth in his grey eyes as he looked down at her, and she frowned as he ruffled her hair. “I missed you, Bronwyn.”

Shock and heat rolled through her as she saw in his eyes that he meant that, that he had been thinking about her while they had been apart and that he had missed her.

He stilled, his hand lingering in her hair, his eyes locked with hers.

She tried to think of something to say as he shifted his gaze to his hand and then back to meet hers, an awkward look blooming in his eyes, as if he had just realised what he had done and what he had said.

Felt that he had said too much.

When he hadn’t said nearly enough.

She needed to know how he felt about her, needed to know if he would ever come to look at her as a woman, someone he could love, or whether he would always view her as a sister.

“I better hit the shower.” He backed away from her, his hand slipping from her hair, and turned before she could stop him. “Swing by later. We’ll talk about your trouble.”

Bronwyn stared at his back as he hurried across the steppingstones, making a fast exit.

The trouble she really needed to talk about was something she couldn’t discuss with him.

Rune was right.

Maverick was her fated male.

CHAPTER 8

Maverick had been on edge since he had made the mistake of going to see Bronwyn. He should have continued to his cabin and cleaned himself off and dressed, should have done any number of things differently rather than going straight to her. The way she had looked at him, openly eyeing his body with a flicker of heat in her eyes, had set his blood on fire and roused a wild need inside him, one that had threatened to steal control of him more than once.

That hunger had only worsened when he had touched her hair. The feel of the silken strands against his palm was branded on his mind now, had been filling his head with thoughts of sifting his fingers through the gold and chestnut strands. How would she have reacted? Would she have welcomed his caress?

He swigged his beer—his second of the night. The first he had downed in a heartbeat, needing to take the edge off. A shot of whiskey had preceded that beer. Drinking wasn't going to solve anything though. He still couldn't stop thinking about her, couldn't shut down that part of his mind that was fixed on her, or the part of him that was constantly waiting for her to make an appearance.

Rune was saying something, and he tried to focus on his friend, tried to pay attention to the conversation he was supposed to be having with him and Callie, but the whole of him was locked on the world around him, his senses stretched as far as he could reach them.

Waiting.

His heart drummed hard; a pounding beat that filled his ears and echoed nerves he couldn't shake.

Callie swept her hand over Rune's shoulder, fingers lightly stroking his muscles through his black T-shirt. The two of them were dressing like a couple these days, preferring a matching jeans and T-shirt combo.

Rune glanced down at her legs. "I'm still calling that a crime against good jeans."

The wolf looked down at her black denim shorts and pulled a face. "I like them. It's not like it's the only pair of jeans I had."

"I bought them. I should get a say in their fate," Rune grunted.

Callie rolled her amber eyes, sighed and looked at Maverick. "What do you think of them?"

Maverick held his hands up. "I have no opinion. I don't want to get into a fight tonight. No way I'm looking at your legs."

"You wouldn't cut your jeans into shorts?" She glanced at his legs, earning a growl from her mate.

"Gods, no." Maverick frowned at her and took another long pull on his beer. He tended to feel the cold, preferred to keep himself wrapped up, even in summer. Shorts were out of the question.

"Amen to that." Rune tilted his beer towards Maverick and tapped it against his bottle.

Callie pulled a face. "You two are far too similar at times. You're sure you're not brothers?"

Rune chuckled and it was good to hear his friend laughing again, to see that bright spark in his eyes and how happy he was.

Maverick finished his second beer and went for a third, drifting away from Rune and Callie, towards the group gathered around the grill. Callie would blend right in with them. Every single one of them was wearing shorts of some fashion, the blond twin bears pairing their cargo shorts with black T-shirts while Skye wore a faded grey tank with small blue denim shorts and Cameo had a sensible cream tee on that went well with her khaki hiking shorts, and made her look every bit the ranger she was.

Lowe was at the helm as always, a smile in his blue eyes and a beer in his hand as he snapped tongs at Cameo, making his mate giggle and try to evade him. The blond bear didn't relent as she hid behind Skye, causing the petite brunette to frown at Lowe.

Knox snatched the tongs from his twin's grip, his grin wicked. "I'm going to do the grilling for once."

"Good gods, no." Lowe was quick to launch at his younger brother, making a valiant attempt to reclaim the tongs.

Cameo and Skye burst into laughter as the two of them chased each other around the grill.

Maverick shook his head and sighed, nodded to Saint as he emerged from his cabin with Holly plastered to his side. Another two victims of the shorts trend. The sight of his alpha in a pair of knee-length black cargo shorts was disturbing. He wasn't sure he had ever seen Saint in shorts before.

He did his best not to look at Holly directly, noticed that Lowe and Knox did the same, diligently keeping their eyes off her. Maverick wasn't a cub. If he looked at Holly in her small shorts and bikini top, Saint would explode. His alpha already looked on edge, was flicking glances at all the males.

Holly pressed closer to her mate, her hand brushing his chest through his dark T-shirt as she said something to him, her whole face lighting up with it. The two of them were inseparable. Maverick glanced at the other couples. In fact, all of them rarely left each other's sides. He was starting to feel like a fifth wheel.

He glanced in the direction of the cabin where Bronwyn was staying before he could stop himself.

Unfortunately, it meant he was looking right at Rune.

His friend's blue eyes narrowed with his frown and then his features relaxed and he glanced over his shoulder. When Rune's gaze came back to him, it was warm, soft with understanding that Maverick wanted to pretend didn't exist. It was easier that way. The last thing he needed was Rune getting ideas about him having feelings for Bronwyn, even if that was the truth.

Maverick grabbed another two bottles of beer, feeling he was going to need them if he was going to make it through tonight. Running had made him feel better, but this time it had only lasted until he had walked back into Black Ridge and felt Bronwyn's eyes on him.

His whole body had lit up the second her gaze had landed on him, his blood rushing faster, heart pounding in a way that had unsettled him. He had fought in cages for decades, had faced countless foes in that time, but he had never felt as nervous as she made him with only a look.

He downed one of the beers, tossed the empty in the pail near the grill, and grabbed another.

"You good?" Saint rumbled as he paused close to him, concern shining in his dark eyes. Holly tiptoed and he leaned towards her, his expression softening as she pressed a kiss to his whiskered cheek, and then she bounced away from him, heading for Skye and Cameo. Saint stared at the back of her head, or more specifically, the mating mark on her nape that she had revealed by twisting her black hair up into a messy knot. Maverick went to move away, but Saint caught his arm. "I asked if you were good."

Maverick shrugged, rolling his shoulders beneath his black cable-knit sweater. "I'm fine."

He wasn't.

He really wasn't.

He had been going in circles for hours, torn between polar feelings, and between twin needs. Part of him had wanted to go and see Bronwyn, and the rest of him had wanted to head to the lodge and stay the hell away from her. She deserved better. He felt that all the way to his soul. Rune could deal with her trouble for her. It would be better that way.

The look Rune gave him when he glanced at his friend warned him that it wasn't going to happen. Rune would make him stay, and as much as he hated to admit it, as deeply as he wanted to run from this, his friend was right. He couldn't do that to Bronwyn. She needed help, needed protection, and something deep inside him wouldn't let him walk away and let someone else take care of her.

"Your run didn't help?" Saint's deep voice rolled over him, pulling him back to his alpha.

Maverick shook his head.

Saint looked worried by that, closed the distance between them and placed a hand on his shoulder, squeezing it gently. "This something I should be worried about too?"

When his alpha flicked a glance towards the other side of the creek, Maverick was quick to shake his head again, because he knew Saint. If Saint believed Bronwyn was a threat to his pride, that she was going to place them in danger, he would be quick to remove her from the property. He couldn't let that happen. He couldn't leave her undefended like that. Vulnerable. If she was right and she did have hunters on her tail, then she needed strong fighters around her, people who could handle them. She wasn't a fighter.

She was too kind. Too gentle. Had a good heart, one that didn't deserve to be stained with blood.

Holly came bounding back to her mate, looped her arm around his other one and waggled a bottle of beer at him. Saint took it with a smile and her grey-green eyes landed on Maverick. A frown wrinkled her nose.

"Don't you ever wear something that suits the season more?" She waved her hand around, towards the deep blue sky. "It's summer."

Maverick shrugged again.

Saint freed his arm from her grip and settled it around her shoulders, tucking her against his side. "Mav feels the cold more than most of us. It's just the way he is. Not all of us can run around in shorts and a bikini top in twenty degrees Celsius weather."

"I'd pay to see Maverick in shorts and a bikini top." Holly's eyes gained a mischievous glint.

Maverick was quick to move a step back from his alpha, had placed some distance between them before Saint had even growled at him, flashing fangs in his direction.

Saint swept Holly up into his arms, ripping a shriek from her, and marched her towards their cabin. "That's it. I'm putting more clothes on you, before I'm tempted to peel off what you are wearing or murder someone."

Maverick made his way to the firepit that stood to the right of that cabin, picked up the iron and podded the blazing logs, his gaze locked on the flames, his mind wandering again. It didn't go far. It drifted to the female every inch of him was waiting to see again, a female he couldn't have, and he tried to shut out the sounds of everyone as they passed the evening with their mates.

Rune came up to stand beside him and Maverick kept his gaze on the fire, avoiding him.

"You need to talk?" Rune lifted his beer to his lips and took a long draught of it.

Maverick shook his head.

"I need to run… or fight… or do something." He closed his eyes, tossed the iron onto the pebbly ground and pinched the bridge of his nose. "I don't know what I need."

"I do," Rune murmured.

Maverick tensed and resisted the temptation to look at his friend. If he didn't look at him, then he didn't have to acknowledge that Rune knew what had him tied in knots. He could keep on pretending that everything hadn't just become complicated, that the path he was on didn't have a split ahead of him, and he didn't need to decide which route he was going to take.

Rune sighed. "Maverick—"

He cut himself off and Maverick knew why.

He had sensed her too.

He turned and dropped his hand from his face, opened his eyes and fixed them on the point beyond Saint's cabin.

Bronwyn came into view there, tentatively glancing around her, looking so uncertain that a need to go to her blasted through him, shook him to his core and had him taking a step towards her. He locked his body up tight, resisting that urge. It wasn't difficult as he stared at her, as the sight of her hit him hard, stunning him.

Gods, she was beautiful.

She swallowed and lifted her left hand, nervously tucked one of the haphazard strands of her pixie cut behind her ear, and then smiled wider than he had ever seen her smile when Callie hurried over to her. The black-haired wolf tucked Bronwyn close to her side, and Bronwyn's honey-coloured eyes lit up as she said something, as Callie ushered her towards the group who had all stopped to look at her.

Bronwyn's gaze shifted to him as everyone greeted her, branded her name on his soul as a flicker of nerves lit her eyes and she toyed with her hair again. She said something to the group and stepped away from them.

Heading for him.

Maverick's heart raced, every fibre of his being deeply aware of her as she walked towards him, her curvy hips swaying in her tight jeans and the loose lower half of her burgundy top fluttering around her stomach in the gentle breeze. She toyed with her hair again, hooking it behind her left ear, the shy way she glanced at him hitting him hard.

Making him nervous.

Her gaze lowered to the ground as she neared him and Rune, an awkward edge to her.

"Damn, Winnie. You grew up beautiful. Didn't she, Maverick?" Rune nudged him.

Maverick tensed and his eyes darted to Rune, and then to her. He hesitated when her gaze met his, his tongue getting tangled, and a hint of a frown formed on her brow and she looked away from him.

He cursed himself. What was he doing? Even better, what was Rune doing? The male was up to something, knew something, and Maverick didn't like it. He stared at Bronwyn, tried not to but couldn't convince himself to look anywhere else. If he was being honest with himself, he would say right that moment maturing hadn't suddenly made her pretty.

She had always been beautiful to him.

He didn't have the balls though.

Swigged his beer in silence instead.

"I think I hear Callie calling. You two will be all right on your own for a while?" Rune gave Bronwyn a look, one that had Maverick feeling uneasy again. Again? He hadn't stopped feeling uneasy from the moment Bronwyn had called him.

"Um." Bronwyn lifted her hand but Rune was already walking away from them. She glanced at Maverick, the nerves he could see in her eyes trickling through him too.

Maverick searched for something to say, something very safe and unlikely to give away anything he was feeling.

His gaze snagged on the pendant hanging around her neck and he frowned at it, was moving before he could stop himself. He took hold of the heart locket, his blood thundering, rage curling through him. Who had given it to her? A lover?

Awareness slowly rolled up on him as he glared at it.

Awareness of her eyes on his face.

Of the tremulous beat of her heart.

Of the nerves he could feel in her.

And how close he was to her, how his knuckles brushed her chest as he held the locket in his fingers, how her scent swirled around him, intoxicating him and making his head hazy as it roused something fierce inside him.

His gaze shifted up a few inches.

To her mouth.

Those sweet rosy lips beckoned him.

CHAPTER 9

Bronwyn's cheeks flushed as Maverick stared at her mouth, lost in thoughts of kissing her. He blinked and panicked a little, felt the need to do something so she didn't get the wrong impression and ended up opening the locket.

He stared at the photograph inside it and blurted, "You were a chubby baby."

She snatched it from him, her fingers brushing his, sending a thousand volts of electricity arcing up his arm. "It's not me. It's my brother."

Her scowl melted away as she turned it towards her and gazed down at it, her mood shifting towards sombre again.

"The locket was my mother's. When the—" She drew down a deep, shuddering breath and he wanted to grip her shoulders, wanted to pull her into his arms and hold her and tell her she didn't have to talk about it, because he couldn't bear to see her hurting. She sighed and angled her head, a hint of a smile curling her lips before it faded again and her emotions swayed back towards hurt. "When the hunters raided our pride… When they grabbed me, the chain snapped. I thought it was lost forever. After Saint and the others freed us, and I went home, I found it waiting on my nightstand. My aunt had found it."

"Your aunt?" He frowned at that. "You never mentioned you had family other than your brother."

She nodded and glanced up at him, and then her gaze fell to the locket again. She stroked her finger over the other photograph it contained, a faded one of a smiling couple.

"Maverick, these are my parents." She angled the locket towards him. "Mom, Dad, this is Maverick. You would have liked him."

He doubted that.

Didn't stop his heart from softening though, turning to mush in his chest as she fondly gazed at the picture, her brow slightly furrowed.

"How long ago did you lose them? Was it during the raid?" He peered at the picture. She looked like her mother, had that same kind air about her and big beguiling eyes, and a bright smile.

Bronwyn shook her head. "It was long before that. I was twenty-six… twenty-seven maybe when they were killed in an avalanche. We had no family left at that pride, so the alpha shipped me and my brother off to live with our aunt and cousin in Whistler."

He flexed his fingers and curled them into fists, battling the desire to brush them across her cheek when tears lined her dark eyelashes and he knew they weren't only about her parents. She was thinking about her brother too.

"Do you remember anything about them?" Maverick glanced at the photo again.

She shook her head. "Not really. I was so young and it was so long ago. My aunt tells me stories about them. She's my mother's younger sister. Are your parents still alive?"

He was quick to shake his head too when she looked at him, swigged his beer and cleared his throat as feelings he had thought he had buried long ago made it feel too tight. "They were killed in a raid on our pride forty years ago."

"The one that brought you to the compound?" Her golden eyes softened as they held his.

He nodded, gulped down another mouthful of beer, and then blew out his breath. When he had arrived at the compound, Rune had asked about his family, and Maverick remembered he had bluntly told the male they were dead. He hadn't shed a tear for them. He hadn't been a good son, or a good kid. He had given them so much trouble when they had done their hardest to wrangle him under control, to stop him from fighting every bear who so much as looked at him in the wrong way.

He never had been a good male.

But he had never felt it more keenly than he did at that moment as he looked at Winnie, wanting something he knew he couldn't have.

She dropped her gaze back to her pendant. "I guess my aunt and my cousin are like a mom and a sister to me. Andrew never got along with them. He never got along with anyone at the pride. I think that's why… I think…"

Her throat worked on a hard swallow and he couldn't stop himself from touching her arm when he sensed the shift in her emotions.

Bronwyn sniffled and snapped the locket closed. "I think that's why the pride didn't fight harder to protect us when the hunters came."

The need to pull her into his arms was strong, battering him, and he almost crumbled. She pulled away from him though, chuckled mirthlessly and shrugged it off. There was no point in her pretending that the actions of her pride hadn't hurt her. It was written all over her face when she looked at him, and now he knew why she had looked so miserable when she had arrived at the compound.

She had craved a family and had thought she had found it, and her brother had ruined it for her.

"Your aunt and this cousin love you though. I'm guessing they do anyway. You look happy when you talk about them." He held his nerve and refused to look away when she stared deep into his eyes, hers widening slightly.

Because he noticed little things about her?

It wasn't as if he could be any other way when it came to her. He didn't mean to, but he had always studied her closely, had always been attuned to her, aware of even the smallest change in her feelings.

"They do. It's… been nice living with them." She lightly boxed him on his arm, lingered with her knuckles against it as her expression softened again. "I missed you and Rune though."

Gods, he had missed her too.

Ached inside even now, when she was standing before him.

So close to him, but so far beyond his reach.

He searched for something to say as she gazed up at him, deeply aware of how close she was to him as his blood thundered, as that uneasiness flowed through him again, tearing him in two. What was it about this female that had him speechless all the time, unable to so much as look at her without feeling tied in knots?

He wasn't sure he was equipped to handle the way she made him feel.

It was all new to him, but at the same time, it wasn't.

And that scared him.

Together with how she looked at him, as if he was some kind of saviour, a male who deserved her attention.

He was far from being both of those things.

And that was his problem.

The cages and the compound might be in his rear view, but that didn't change who he was or the things he had done. He wasn't a good male. He wasn't gentle. Kind. If she knew the kind of beast he was, she would run and not look back.

But that wasn't the reason he needed to keep his distance from her.

Hell, maybe it would be better if she did know.

Maybe it would be better if he told her right now about the kind of male he was. He could paint a black picture of how he was with females, could tell her how brutal he could be in the heat of the moment, when a side of himself that he wasn't proud of came to the fore to steal control. He could make her see the kind of male she was dealing with and she would leave.

And it would be for the best.

Because she was gentle, sweet, delicate, and far too innocent to belong to a monster like him.

"Maverick?" Her soft voice curled around him, teasing his ears, making him ache to tug her to him and at the same time burn with a need to push her away, to keep her safe.

To protect her.

From himself.

"He spacing out again?" Rune tapped a cold bottle against Maverick's left temple.

Earning himself a growl.

He slid a black look at Rune, who looked unrepentant.

"I think so." Bronwyn looked worried now as she glanced between him and Rune.

Rune shoved the beer at him. "Here. Drink up."

Maverick snatched it and downed the old one he was holding, grimacing at how warm it was.

"Come on. Let's get you a drink." Callie tugged on Bronwyn's arm, stealing her away from him, and Maverick wasn't surprised when Rune followed them.

He breathed a little easier as the distance between them grew and wrestled with his out-of-control feelings as he swigged the ice-cold beer Rune had given him. Doing his damnedest not to look at Bronwyn. He needed to get his head on straight when it came to her, but he wasn't sure he ever would, not now that he had realised a few things.

Like the fact he was crazy about her.

Saint strolled over to him, a warm look in his dark eyes that made Maverick want to sigh, because apparently everyone wanted to coddle him tonight. It wasn't like the big brunet bear to make a fuss like this. Hell, it wasn't like Rune to make a fuss over him either, and that was exactly what his friend was doing in his own way.

"How are you doing?" Saint stopped beside him and turned to face the same direction, so they stood shoulder to shoulder.

Maverick didn't want to think about the answer to that question, so he grunted, "Fine."

Felt his alpha slide him a look.

"I know you, Maverick. We all do. You can grunt and deflect all you want, but there's no mistaking you're not in a good place."

Not in a good place.

That felt like the understatement of the century.

He took a long pull on his beer.

"I think I just need to run again." His gaze shifted to his cabin where it stood a few hundred feet away, near to Rune's cabin, and beyond it, to the head of the valley and the glacier there. "Maybe hit up the lodge for a few days… or maybe just keep running this time."

Saint's sigh said it all. "Running doesn't solve anything. It won't change anything. In my experience, it only tends to make things worse."

Maverick slid his gaze back to Bronwyn, deeply aware that his alpha was right and there was no running from his feelings for her. It wouldn't change anything. It would only leave her vulnerable, without him there to protect her, to help her.

He barely bit back the growl that rumbled in his chest as Knox handed Bronwyn a beer, the too-handsome blond grizzly flashing her a wide smile as she hesitated to take it. She waved him away, an apologetic look on her face, and then crumbled and took the long neck bottle.

When she swigged it, she pulled a face, and everyone laughed.

Fire swept through his blood when she looked wounded, had him on the verge of crossing the clearing to her and beating the crap out of Knox and the others, but then she smiled and laughed too.

Captivating him.

"How long have you known her?" Saint's deep voice rumbled in his ears as Maverick gazed at her, bewitched all over again, unable to tear his gaze away from her as she smiled and tried the beer again.

She didn't grimace as badly this time.

"Only for five years or so. She didn't arrive long before you and the others freed us." Maverick almost smiled as Holly said something and Bronwyn's whole face lit up, her smile bright enough to illuminate the world.

Hell, it illuminated his, chasing back the darkness in his soul and the shadows from this world, making everything look different—better.

She cast a look in his direction, lingered when she found him looking at her, and hooked her hair behind her ear again. Rune said something, stealing her attention away from Maverick, and she talked to him, and it felt good to see her so animated, so happy, as if all the weight of her troubles had been lifted from her heart.

"I want to know about this trouble she's in," Saint said.

Maverick nodded. "She mentioned hunters in Whistler and that she felt sure they had recognised her, and she believes they might have taken her brother."

"Doesn't sound good. Have you managed to get anything else out of her?"

He shook his head. "I haven't had the chance to speak with her about it."

Saint nodded towards her. "Bring her over. I want to talk to her."

Maverick wanted to growl at the male, the need to protect Bronwyn rising inside him as he caught the look in Saint's dark eyes, one that said his alpha had no intention of being nice and gentle with her. He didn't want to talk to her. He wanted to interrogate her.

The thought of subjecting her to a grilling when she had just started smiling and laughing, had begun to look as if she was more at ease, rankled and he barely leashed the urge to bare fangs at Saint and tell him to back off. He didn't want to kill that smile.

He didn't want to extinguish that bright light in her eyes and he knew he would if he dragged her before his alpha.

He tried to put himself in Saint's position, told himself on repeat that his alpha was only trying to protect his pride. He couldn't be furious with Saint when he'd had the same feeling about Bronwyn, a sense that something wasn't right and she wasn't telling him the whole truth about her situation.

Maverick forced himself to trudge across the clearing, swore he would stick by her side and make sure Saint wouldn't cross a line with her as he closed the distance between them.

"You should eat something. How about a sausage?" Skye swept her chestnut braids over her shoulder and grabbed the tongs from Lowe. She snapped them as she ran them along the line of sausages on the grill, her face lighting up with a wicked smile as she settled on one. "I have just the one for you, Bronwyn. It's big and a little dark. Think you can handle it?"

She grabbed the sausage and turned towards Bronwyn, who giggled. He had never seen Winnie laugh like this, and it hit him hard. He thought about how tough things had been for her—for all of them—and how different she seemed now. So normal.

And he was glad.

Skye spotted him and locked up tight, still holding the sausage aloft.

Bronwyn frowned at her and then turned to see what she was looking at, and the moment her eyes landed on him, she blushed. Hard.

He hadn't been born yesterday, knew Skye had been making a filthy innuendo with the sausage, no doubt trying to link it with him in order to make Bronwyn blush. As the only unmated pair at the Ridge, it was expected that they would be the source of entertainment for the others, but he still didn't appreciate it.

He glowered at Skye and she was quick to toss the sausage back on the grill.

"Lighten up," Knox muttered. "It was a perfectly innocent offer of sausage."

Winnie's cheeks went so red that she looked like a tomato.

He had never seen her so embarrassed, and the fact it was over him had his blood racing, the nerves he had managed to vanquish returning.

Callie held another beer out to Bronwyn.

Maverick intercepted it. "Saint wants to talk."

The light in Bronwyn's eyes faded.

"Uh oh." Skye grabbed another beer from the pail and shoved it towards her. "You might need this!"

Winnie was quick to take it. Maverick scowled at Skye. The female was trouble. He gave Knox a look that told him to keep his mate under control, but Knox shrugged it off.

Maverick pivoted on his heel and followed Bronwyn as she bravely strode towards Saint where he waited by the firepit, sticking close to her so she didn't feel nervous about talking with him.

Thankfully, Holly had joined her mate, already had the hard edge smoothed off his expression as she spoke to him and lightly stroked his arm. Saint's dark eyes shifted to Bronwyn as she stopped before him, keeping a few feet between them, and he silently thanked his alpha for waiting for him to reach her before he started with the questions.

"Maverick said you have hunter trouble. Something about you feeling they have your brother?"

She nodded, lifted her hand and stroked her fingers over the locket. "I told Maverick he's been going to Vancouver more frequently recently and this time he didn't come back, and then I saw those hunters in Whistler. I'm worried about him. Andrew isn't… He's not the strongest bear."

Maverick wanted to put in that he really wasn't. Andrew was one of the rare males who had been assigned to clean up duties and working in the mess hall rather than being made to fight. The hunters had taken pity on him.

Probably because he had literally pissed himself when they had put him in the cage, and it had only been a training match.

Andrew also hadn't been the best of brothers to Winnie. Maverick wouldn't be surprised if the male had just gotten caught up in the buzz of Vancouver.

Hell, he had been there and done that.

Whenever he and Rune went there for winter, it was like stepping into a completely different world, one that was enticing and bewitching. It always took him some time to readjust to the quietness of Black Ridge when he returned in spring, but he preferred it here. Vancouver was nice for a while, but this was where he felt at home. At peace.

He wasn't sure he could say the same of her brother. When they had been at the compound, Andrew had often talked of the city. He hated to think that the male might have decided to stay there this time, might have been caught up in the excitement of it and just forgotten to call his sister, leaving her afraid for him.

"I told Maverick I shouldn't come here, in case the hunters are following me." Her voice was small, holding a note of fear that had Maverick wanting to step closer to her to reassure her.

Saint slid him a black look. "I'm inclined to agree, but you're here now. We'll help any way we can. I can get in touch with my contacts, see if they know of any compounds in the area."

"Really?" Her eyes lit up. "That would be… I'm not sure what to say. Thank you?"

"Don't thank me yet. Archangel clamped down on the illegal arenas a few years back. If hunters did capture your brother, chances are they weren't rogue and they've taken him to the Vancouver headquarters." Saint's tone was grave and Maverick kept a close eye on Winnie.

This was going to hit her hard.

She blanched. "No. I mean… no. They couldn't have. If they took him there—"

She didn't need to say any more than that. Everyone knew what fate awaited anyone who was taken to an official Archangel building. *Studying*. Which was the Archangel way of saying experimenting on and torturing non-humans, usually until they were dead.

Bronwyn swallowed thickly. "I… I don't feel so good."

She turned and hurried away from them, and rather than heading for the group near the grill, she made a beeline for the space between the rear of Saint's cabin and the outbuilding that stood in the centre of the clearing. When she disappeared into the darkness, the urge to go after her was strong.

Maverick told himself not to follow, but he was powerless to stop himself. He hurried after her, catching up with her near the creek, where she had stopped. Her head was bent, her back to him. What was she doing?

He cautiously moved around her and frowned when he found her staring at her locket, at the photographs it contained. The moon cast pale light on them and on her, threading her chestnut hair with silver. He stepped closer to her, lifted his left hand and flexed his fingers, hesitating only a moment before he placed it against her back. Her bare skin was cold beneath his palm, but soft too, had him aching to gather her into his arms to warm her and feel her pressed against him.

"You okay?" he murmured.

She sniffed and nodded, swigged her beer and then looked up at him.

The tears lining her lashes hit him hard.

He frowned at her, his brow furrowing as he searched for something to say.

The words came easily this time.

"I'm sure Andrew is fine. He's probably just got caught up in Vancouver and forgot to call you." His words felt hollow as they left his lips, and how was he meant to make her believe them when he didn't believe them himself?

She shook her head, her face crumpling. "I know he's not fine. I know it. Hunters have him."

He wouldn't be surprised if they did, or if the hunters were targeting her too now to keep him in line. Saint didn't believe there were any arenas left on this side of Canada, but Maverick did. Archangel might have shut some down, but it would have only made the rogue hunters who ran them more cautious, more careful about keeping their wretched business secret from their superiors. That business was far too lucrative to stop hunters from finding a way to make an arena happen and to keep it open.

Winnie swallowed another mouthful of beer, lowered the bottle and wiped her eyes, and then took another long draught.

She sighed, her look despondent as she stared at the creek, her brow furrowed and shoulders sagging. "They have him… and gods only know what they're doing to him. I'm so scared, Maverick."

He stepped towards her, every instinct he possessed demanding he comfort her, hijacking control to have him sliding his arm around her shoulders and tugging her against his side. "We'll get him back, Winnie. I promise."

She looked up at him, her gaze soft, bewitching him all over again as moonlight bathed her skin.

"Thank you," she whispered.

His gaze fell to her lips, his thoughts turning to kissing her. She was so close to him. He only had to dip his head and he could know the taste of her. His fingers tensed against her shoulder and he caught himself, released her instead. She frowned as he moved a step away from her and he tilted his head back, pretending he had wanted to look at the stars.

Shutting down his unruly desires.

She swigged her beer again, wobbled a little as she walked away from him, a sigh escaping her. She tipped her head up and her mouth fell open as she gazed at the heavens.

"So many stars," she murmured and he frowned at the slight slur of the final word.

Looked at her.

His frown intensified as she slowly turned, her eyes still on the sky, her motions wobbly. It wasn't the uneven pebbly shore that had had her wobbling as she walked. It was the beer.

He huffed, strode over to her and snatched the bottle from her. "That's enough of that. You, Winnie, are a bit of a lightweight."

She giggled and dropped her head, hit him with a grin that had his stupid heart skipping a beat. "I've never had alcohol before. Does it always make you feel like this?"

"Like what?" He tried to figure out how many beers she'd had before he had cut her off.

She sidled closer, her voice dropping to a sultry whisper. "Bold. A little reckless. A lot wild."

Maverick swallowed hard.

Gods, he wanted to kiss her when she looked at him like that, as if she really wanted him.

"I think you should call it a night." He also thought he should move back a step as she advanced on him, but he couldn't convince his damned feet to cooperate.

Her eyes grew hooded, her look far too sexy.

He muttered, "You really can't handle your drink."

Shook off the part of him that was roaring at him to kiss her.

He took hold of her arm and ignored her little gasp that teased his ears, because he wasn't going to surrender to the urge to kiss her. She was drunk. He was damned if he was going to take advantage of her.

He paused and looked at her. It hit him that he was different around her.

Back in the day, at the arena, plenty of inebriated females had come on to him, and he had never turned them down after a fight. He had never cared that they were drunk. But he cared that she was.

The thought of kissing her when she wasn't fully in control of herself, when her inhibitions had been stripped away by beer, didn't sit well with him at all.

“Come on.” He tugged her towards the river, doing his best to ignore how her gaze set him on fire as it lingered on his profile, or how she placed her hand over his and stroked his fingers in a maddening way.

Maverick lifted her onto the steppingstones and waded through the river beside her, helping her across the gaps between the boulders. By helping, he meant lifting her from one to the next, touching her curvy waist only as long as was necessary to get her to the other side of the creek without her falling into it.

He set her down on the bank when they reached it and marched her to the door of her cabin, opened it for her and waited for her to go inside when he released her.

She turned and pressed her hands to his chest.

And kissed him.

Heat flooded Maverick, her peaches and cream taste driving him wild in an instant, rousing a fierce hunger inside him that had him kissing her back as he wrapped his arms around her and pulled her against him. She yielded to him, slid her arms around his neck and opened to him, and he growled as he angled his head and deepened the kiss, every inch of him on fire, his heart thundering as his tongue stroked hers. He backed her against the doorframe, pressed her there as he claimed her mouth, itching to claim far more than that.

When she moaned, he saw a flash of her on her back on a table in a sterile holding room, spread before him as he pounded into her.

Maverick gripped her hips and shoved her back as he wrenched himself away from her, was quick to release her as he breathed hard.

Her wide eyes locked with his.

Innocent. Far too innocent.

He couldn’t taint her.

He wasn’t the angel she thought he was and if she knew the things he had done, how he had treated females while caught up in the high of being crowned the victor in a cage fight, she would look at him differently.

Like the demon he really was.

Maverick turned on his heel and walked away from her.

CHAPTER 10

Bronwyn stretched and smiled as she woke, savoured the warmth of the blankets and sank into the mattress, feeling relaxed from head to toe. She idly twirled a lock of hair around her fingers as sleep gradually fell away from her. Why did she feel so sated this morning? Maybe she'd had a delicious dream of Maverick again.

She licked her lips as it came back to her, wanted to moan as she recalled how bruising his kiss had been, how it had felt as if he was claiming her with the hard press of his mouth against hers and his hands firmly gripping her backside.

Her eyes snapped open. She shot up in bed. Cursed when it hit her that it hadn't been a dream. She had kissed Maverick.

A blush burned up her cheeks, seemed to set every inch of her aflame. Oh gods. She'd had far too many beers and then she had kissed him, had practically thrown herself at him. She groaned and rolled, buried her head under the pillow and curled into a foetal position on her side. What had she done?

Her heart pounded, loud in her ears as she remembered the kiss, how delicious it had been at first.

And then Maverick had pushed her away from him and had looked at her as if she was pure evil.

He hadn't been able to get away from her fast enough.

Bronwyn groaned again, her face screwing up. Maybe if she stayed here, under this pillow, and never saw him again he would forget what she had done. She knew in her heart that hiding from him wasn't going to solve anything though. Sooner or later, either he or Rune would come to check on her. Gods, she hoped Rune came, but she wasn't sure she could even face him. He would say that he had told her so, would point out what had become blindingly apparent to her last night.

Maverick was definitely her fated male.

The beer had loosened her up enough that she had forgotten the nerves she normally felt around him, had felt bold and maybe a little beautiful, and it was his fault. The way he had looked at her had revealed he wanted her. He hadn't needed to say a word. It had been right there in his eyes.

His kiss had revealed just how deeply that want ran.

And then he had pulled away, had left without a word, and now she wasn't sure what to think.

Had she been reading into things, seeing something that wasn't there thanks to the beer, or did Maverick really desire her? She wasn't a fool. He hid it well, but he had never been able to hide from her that he had a low opinion of himself. She had only known him a handful of years, but in that time, she had witnessed things about him that she knew were a source of shame for him.

And she knew deep in her heart that was the reason he had stopped things last night.

The look he had given her—the one that called her evil—hadn't really been aimed at her. It had been aimed at himself. He had thought himself a monster for kissing her like that, for holding her so tightly, for changing things between them.

And they were changed.

She couldn't go back to how things had been. There was no way to undo the past. She could blame it on the beer, they both could, but it would be a lie. She wanted him, always had and always would.

She loved him.

Bronwyn tossed the pillow aside and huffed as she rolled onto her back, debating what to do. Finding Maverick would be a good place to start, and while she was doing that she would make a decision about what she did next.

Apologise or kiss him again. She wasn't sure.

Her head ached as she shifted her legs over the edge of the mattress and stood, and she pressed her hand to it and frowned. Last night, beer had been amazing, the best thing ever. In the cold light of morning, beer sucked.

She pulled her jeans and camisole on, and then a purple sweater one of the females had dropped off for her. The air was chilly again this morning, had her hurrying down the stairs to the log burner to get it going. She made fast work of cleaning it out and building a fire, latched the door and stood, her gaze scanning the room. She must have left her boots somewhere.

Bronwyn frowned when she found one by the far end of the room and spotted the other near the door.

Grimaced when she recalled removing them in anger after Maverick had walked away from her and throwing them when frustration had got the better of her.

She grabbed them and tugged them on, and opened the door, her mind on finding Maverick and probably apologising.

She almost jumped out of her skin when her phone rang.

Bronwyn turned away from the open door and looked for it, following the jaunty tune. It wasn't on the couch. Her pulse raced, heart hammering against her ribs as fear trickled through her veins, swiftly building into a torrent that left her breathless. It was the hunters. She knew it. She hurried upstairs to the loft bedroom and found it on the nightstand.

Grabbed it.

It went silent.

Damn it.

She stared at the screen, trembling badly, unsure whether she wanted them to call back again or leave her alone. Jumped when it rang again.

She hit the answer button. "Hello?"

"I thought I was going to have to punish your brother there for a moment." The familiar female voice hit her hard.

Bronwyn frowned when the line crackled, pulled it from her ear and looked at the signal bars. They were non-existent. If she wasn't careful, she would lose this call.

And probably her brother with it.

"I want to talk to him," she said, aware she wasn't in a position to make demands, but she needed to know her brother was all right. She remembered something else about last night.

Saint had mentioned they might have taken her brother to the Vancouver HQ of Archangel.

She doubted that was the case, but she couldn't stop her mind from conjuring images of Andrew in a cold white room, strapped to a table and being tortured by Archangel scientists as he screamed in pain.

"No." The female continued before Bronwyn could say anything. "Have you secured our assets?"

Bronwyn pressed a hand to her stomach and sagged onto the bed, feeling sick all over again and not because of the hangover. She hated how this woman talked about Rune and Maverick as if they were a possession, something they owned, not living, breathing people.

"I need more time."

"That's unacceptable. Do you want us to hurt your brother?" There was a note in the huntress's voice, one that said she found the thought of hurting Andrew appealing, and Bronwyn tried to shun the images of him on his knees with that hunter looming next to him, a blade poised to cut his throat.

"You're sick," she muttered, tears lining her eyelashes and the bridge of her nose burning. "Don't hurt him. Please? I'm close. I just need a little more time."

"You don't have more time," the huntress snarled. "Either you deliver our assets or we kill your brother."

Bronwyn struggled to hold back her tears as a war erupted inside her, tearing her in two all over again. She couldn't hand Maverick and Rune over to these people, but she couldn't abandon her brother either. What was she supposed to do? Andrew wasn't strong. He wouldn't survive if the hunters pushed him into a cage fight.

Maverick and Rune were strong. They were still fighters. There was a chance they would survive long enough for Saint to rally his allies, the ones he had mentioned kept an eye on the hunters and were still actively looking for compounds. Saint could save them again.

But gods, they would hate her. They would never forgive her.

"It seems you want us to kill your brother. Very well."

"No! Wait. I'll do it." She clutched the phone, hating herself as those words fell from her and she realised that she would. She would put Maverick and Rune through that hell again just to save her brother. She was despicable. As evil as Maverick had called her with that look he had given her last night.

"I think I have their trust now." Those words leaked from her, made her feel worse, as wretched as she really was for doing this to two males she loved, two bears who had taken great care of her and had kept her safe.

"That's good. Bring them to the location I'm going to send you. I don't care what you have to tell them to get them there, just get them to that place by nightfall tomorrow."

Bronwyn swallowed hard. "What if they won't go? What if I need more time?"

The huntress snapped, "You don't have more time. Your brother doesn't have any more time. Either you bring us our assets, or your brother dies. Do you want your brother to die?"

"No." She shook her head.

But then she didn't want Rune and Maverick pushed back into cages either, forced to fight again to entertain the sick bastards who had held them before. She didn't want Maverick to go through that again. He was so different now, so much lighter. He smiled now. She didn't want to kill that smile. It lit up her world. She sighed and sagged, all of her hope rushing from her, because what other choice did she have?

"I'll have them there by dusk tomorrow." She ended the call, her heart heavy as she thought about what she was going to do, as she tried to think of a way to turn this around on the hunters somehow and make sure everyone she loved survived.

Tensed as Maverick's deep voice rolled up the stairs, a black snarl that had her heart shooting into her throat.

"Get who where by dusk tomorrow?"

CHAPTER 11

Maverick was worried about Bronwyn. He had spent all night thinking about her, had lain awake on his bed mulling over that kiss and his past, and tangled in knots about the things he wanted. He wanted her. Plain and simple. Not because she was his fated female, but because he had feelings for her, because she was beautiful and a light in his dark world.

She was everything to him.

He feared he had ruined things with that kiss though. He hadn't been gentle with her, had let his urges get the better of him when he should have been tender, treating her in the way she deserved to be treated. She wasn't one of the females the hunters had rewarded him with whenever he had provided good entertainment. She was soft, and kind, and gods take pity on her, he loved her.

A bend in the track had him snapping his focus back to the forest and watching his footing as he pounded around the corner and followed the path as it dropped sharply into a basin. His legs ached as he pushed himself to keep running. Sweat trickled down his bare back and the chilly kiss of morning air against it did nothing to cool him down.

He wasn't sure how long he had been running.

The second it had been light enough, he had taken off into the woods, had made it to the lodge by the time the sun had peeked above the mountains, threading the fingers of cloud in the sky with gold and pink. He had been tempted to stop there a while, but the need to see Bronwyn had grown to an unbearable level as he had watched the sunrise.

The need to explain things to her had had him turning back around and heading back to Black Ridge. Maybe if he explained some things about himself, she would understand and wouldn't view him as some kind of monster.

Maybe if he let her in so he was no longer afraid of her finding out about the darker side of himself, the one he had kept hidden from her, in the heat of the moment, then he could have a shot at being with her. It might change things. It might change him.

A male could only hope.

She had changed him by degrees, he was aware of that now. From the moment she had walked into his life, he had been gradually changing for the better, had been taking small steps towards becoming a better male, and he hadn't stopped striving to achieve that once they had been separated.

He cursed.

He felt sure that after they had parted he had only tried harder to become something better, someone worthy of her, working towards the day where he felt ready to find her and tell her that he needed her.

Maverick slowed as Black Ridge came into view, his gaze snagging on the smoke that curled from the chimney of her cabin. Thoughts of getting cleaned up and more presentable before he saw her fell to the wayside and he headed towards her cabin rather than his, the need to see her too pressing to ignore.

He kicked off his trainers and waded across the creek upstream from the cabin, gritting his teeth when the frigid water chilled his legs through his sweatpants and numbed his bare feet.

Adrenaline was quick to flow through his racing blood as he thought about what he was going to say to her, unsure whether to dance around things a little to soften the impact or be direct and just lay it all out there. Blunt tended to be his weapon of choice when it came to conversations, but he had the feeling that this talk with Winnie was going to require more finesse if he wanted to emerge from it with his heart intact.

Being blunt with her would probably only drive her away.

Maybe breaking it to her a little at a time would be the best move.

He blew out his breath as he neared the cabin.

Pulled up short when he saw the door was open.

Maverick frowned and eased up the steps, stretched his senses outwards and felt her inside. It was a cold morning for leaving the door open, unless she had been overenthusiastic about building a fire and had made the cabin too hot for her tastes.

He cocked his head as he neared the door and heard her talking.

"I need more time."

More time to do what?

He moved with stealth, listening in on her conversation, curiosity driving him even when he knew it was wrong of him to snoop.

"You're sick," she muttered, her voice tight. "Don't hurt him. Please? I'm close. I just need a little more time."

Her brother. She was talking about her brother. His blood burned at the thought the hunters had called her, had him taking a hard step towards the door, intending to go to her and deal with these hunters for her to spare her the pain.

"No! Wait. I'll do it. I think I have their trust now."

Those words stopped him dead and had alarm bells ringing in his head, that feeling he'd had back when Winnie had called him and asked him to meet her returning. His blood burned for a different reason, hurt swelling in his heart as he glared at the loft bedroom and he recalled what she had told him.

She hadn't just thought hunters had her brother.

She had known they did.

She had known they had him and now it sounded a hell of a lot as if she had always planned to trade him and Rune for her brother. She had been playing him all this time, doing whatever it took to get close to him again and gain his trust.

Intending to lure him into a trap.

Back into that hell.

"What if they won't go? What if I need more time?"

He ignored the hurt he sensed in her, sure it was hurt for her brother, that she was thinking about him, afraid for him.

"No." Her voice was quiet when she added, "I'll have them there by dusk tomorrow."

Maverick stormed to the stairs, his voice a black snarl as rage got the better of him, as the thought that Bronwyn had lied to him, had been playing him, cleaved a hole in his heart.

"Get who where by dusk tomorrow?"

The acrid scent of fear that tainted her fragrance grew stronger and she swept down the stairs, pausing in the bend.

Her wide honey-coloured eyes collided with his. "Maverick."

"Who are you planning to hand over to the hunters, Bronwyn?" he bit out, his mood taking a nosedive as she averted her gaze, confirming his suspicions. Fire blazed through his blood and he took a hard step towards her, his eyes narrowing on her. Anger got the better of him, the pain too much for him to bear, and he barked, "Answer me!"

Her shoulders went rigid and she flinched away from him, and then lurched towards him, pain flashing in her eyes that made him want to scoff at her because she had no damned right to look hurt.

She locked up tight with her hand raised before her when he bared fangs at her, daring her to try to calm him by reaching for him. He wasn't going to fall for her lies again. She eased her hand back towards her chest and tears lined her lashes.

Tears he ignored.

"Yeah. I see how it is now. I should've known better… but maybe I expected better from you. I expected you to be different," he snapped and took another fierce step towards her as rage built inside him, stoking his bear side, making him want to roar at her and shake her, to lash out at her for what she had done. "I thought you gave a fuck about me and Rune, but I was wrong."

She was quick to shake her head. "Maverick—"

"Don't Maverick me. Don't give me that look, like I'm the one at fault." He prowled towards her, breathing hard as his heart thundered, as adrenaline surged and the urge to fight swamped him, clouding his thoughts and making it hard to retain control of himself and resist that black need to lash out. “You’re a liar. You lied to me and Rune. After everything we did for you. How could you?”

Her face crumpled and tears spilled onto her cheeks.

“Spare me the waterworks, Winnie. I’m not going to buy them.” He growled those words and closed the distance between them, lunged for her when anger got the better of him, pushing him to grab her and make her pay for what she had done.

To make her hurt as he was hurting.

She swiftly evaded him, was at the other end of the cabin before his hand cut through thin air where she had been, and he levelled a black look on her.

Her face darkened, her eyebrows knitting hard as the hurt in her eyes grew and anger joined it.

“Hunters have Andrew. I told you they had him. I told you in the only way I could. There was a video call. I saved it on my laptop.” Her hand shook as she pointed towards the closed device on the coffee table and her brow furrowed. “They hurt him, Maverick. They had him in one of those awful cells and a hunter had a knife and cut him and… and… what was I supposed to do?”

“How about tell me about it? That would’ve been a good place to start,” he snarled and advanced on her again, hurt at the thought she had kept this from him mingling with the pain caused by the thought she intended to betray him.

“I couldn’t!” she snapped and then her anger deflated and more tears tracked down her cheeks as she murmured, “I couldn’t. She told me not to. I wasn’t to say a word about it or they would kill him. I just had to do what I was told, and I didn’t know it was you and Rune they were after when they told me to call someone and bring them to a place they would give me later.”

His heart tried to soften, but Maverick steeled it, refusing to let her sway him. As far as he knew, this could all be an act and he had to treat it as one. She was still trying to get him to do as she wanted, trying to lure him into a trap.

"You told me you thought hunters had your brother. Surely that counted as telling me?" Maverick glared at her.

"I was afraid to tell you even that much. I tried to tell you about what was happening in a way I felt wouldn't make them kill my brother. I tried."

He scoffed at that. "We're in the middle of nowhere, Winnie. You could have told us. No one would have known."

"You don't know that!" she barked, her eyes wild as she looked around her. "They could be listening even now. There are things you can do with phones and electronic devices that turn them into microphones for people to listen to… or they could have a drone. This is Archangel we're talking about!"

He hadn't known about the whole listening in through devices thing, but it wasn't an excuse for what she had done.

"There's a thing called pen and paper. You could've written it down. If you cared about me and Rune at—"

Fire flared in her eyes.

"Don't! Don't even talk like that. I was scared, Maverick! I *am* scared. They have my brother and if I don't do this…" The fire in her eyes went out just like that, replaced with hurt and despair that tore at him as she whispered, "I'm sorry. I know I'm being selfish. I'm sorry."

She ran for the door.

No fucking way he was letting her run away from him or from what she had done.

He went after her, caught up with her on the steppingstones and grabbed her when she reached the other side. He growled as he tightened his grip on her arm and yanked her to face him.

"I can't believe you'd do such a thing to me… to Rune… after everything we did for you!" he snarled in her face, his bear side restless and agitated, pushing for control.

Tears streamed down her face as she yelled, "You think I don't feel terrible about this? That this isn't killing me? Rune is like a brother to me and you—"

"Me?" he snapped. "What about me?"

Maverick wanted to know why she had cut herself off, some desperate part of him needing to know how she saw him. As a brother too? Or something else?

"And you…" Her face crumpled again as she tried to twist her arm free, her fight leaving her again. "You're hurting me."

"What the hell is going on?" Rune's deep voice had Winnie trying to look over her shoulder in his direction.

Maverick tugged her back to face him, his fingers pressing into her arm, because he was damned if she was going to look to the black bear for help. She was going to tell him what she had refused to say.

Rune slowed to a walk as he looked at Maverick's hand where he gripped her arm. "Let her go."

Maverick bared fangs at him, warning him to back off. Instinct pressed him to fight the male, to lash out at him and unleash the pent-up aggression that was ripping him apart, had him on the verge of doing something wretched, like hurting the female.

Not just any female.

It was Winnie's arm in his bruising grip.

His beautiful Winnie who had betrayed him and Rune, and was now on the receiving end of his anger.

Rune scowled at his hand and Maverick looked there, saw how fiercely he was holding her, his fingers pressed deep into her skin, bruising her. Gods, he was a monster.

But he couldn't convince himself to release her.

Pain cleaved his heart in two, cut him up into tiny pieces as he looked into her eyes.

"I can't believe you lied to me, Bronwyn. Was everything a lie?" he whispered, useless tears threatening to burn the backs of his eyes as he looked down at her, as the anger in her eyes morphed into hurt that echoed inside him.

She knew what he was asking, and some foolish part of him wanted to believe that look in her eyes that said it hadn't all been a lie—she had meant that kiss.

But he couldn't.

"Release her, Maverick." Saint stopped close to him and when he didn't loosen his hold on her, the big brunet bear grabbed his hand and prised it from her delicate arm. Saint turned to her. "Go to my cabin."

She shook her head, sending tears tumbling down her cheeks, and fought for air as she looked at Maverick, right into his eyes. Her brow furrowed, despair crossing her honey-coloured eyes again, and then she stormed away from him. His gaze tracked her as she headed up the creek.

His heart hurt for a different reason as she sank to her backside near the water, buried her head in her knees, and shook with each heaving sob that wracked her.

A need to go to her filled him.

Maverick resisted it. She had lied to him. She had lied to all of them. She meant his pride harm and he couldn't forgive her for that. Nothing between them had been real.

"Want to explain what that was all about?" Rune took a cautious step towards him.

Maverick pulled down a breath to steady the side of himself that wanted a fight and clenched his fists at his sides. "She lied to us. I heard her talking to hunters. They have her brother and did some video call with her before, gave her my number and that's why she called me. She was going to hand us over to the hunters in exchange for her brother, Rune. Both of us. Back in that hell. She was going to send us back there."

And he hated her for it.

He hated her for hurting him.

He had trusted her and she had betrayed him.

Saint glared at her. "Last night, when I brought up hunters, she looked afraid when we talked about the Archangel HQ in Vancouver. Do you think she knew her brother is being held there?"

Maverick shook his head as he remembered how she had reacted. She had been distraught and now he knew why. She thought her brother was being held there, tortured and experimented on by the hunters.

"She mentioned a cell. Told me that they had shown her brother in one being hurt by a hunter. She was told to call a number and lure them to the hunters, and told not to reveal what she was doing." Maverick huffed as he looked at her, some of his anger abating as she remained with her head buried in her knees as she clung to them. "She claims that she wanted to tell us and she said as much as she could. Made up some crap about drones and thinking Archangel were using her devices to spy on her."

"It's possible." Saint worried his lower lip with his thumb as he frowned at the pebbles. "They could have access to her phone."

"She has a laptop too. Mentioned she saved the video on it." Maverick looked over his shoulder towards the cabin. "It's on the coffee table."

Saint nodded and crossed the creek, leaving him alone with Rune.

Maverick dragged a hand down his face. "I can't believe she did this to us."

"I know you're angry. I'm angry too… but…" Rune looked off to his left, towards Winnie, the hard edge to his expression softening as he gazed at her. "Maybe go a little easier on her? I mean… If she's telling the truth about the video and the hunters… It's her brother, Maverick. What would you do if someone you loved was being held by hunters?"

Maverick hardened his heart, refusing to soften like Rune was. He couldn't forgive her as easily as the black bear. He wouldn't. Her lies and betrayal had cut him too deeply.

"She's been playing me from the start," he growled and glared at her. "From the second I picked up that phone. All those smiles. Those soft looks. That kiss. It was all a fucking lie… an act."

"Winnie kissed you?" Rune's face blackened.

"Last night, when she was drunk… which was probably just another act. She knew exactly what she had been doing… how to make me do whatever she wanted." And it hurt. He was a no-good son of a bitch who got angry too easily and liked fighting far too much, but he wasn't a liar.

He stared at her, feeling as if he no longer knew her. The Bronwyn he had known wouldn't have done this to him. She wouldn't have manipulated someone in such a wretched way, using their feelings against them.

"Maverick," Rune started, stealing his focus away from her.

Maverick frowned when his friend looked torn about something. "What?"

Rune scrubbed a hand over his close-cropped brown hair, heaved a sigh that stretched his black T-shirt tight across his chest, and then dropped his hand to his side.

"I shouldn't say this. It really isn't my place… but Winnie has always had a crush on you." Rune glanced at her, a distant and troubled look in his eyes. "And I think it became something more over the years. She loves you, Maverick."

He could only stare at Rune as those words hit him, as a chill skated down his spine and his mind emptied. Winnie was in love with him? He found that even harder to believe than the fact she had lied to him and had intended to lure him back into the hell of the cages.

Every smile, every look, she had given him over the last few days played out in his mind, from last night to the moment he had set eyes on her again. And then he went further back, recalling the way she had looked at him from time to time when they had been together at the compound.

Remembering how hurt she had looked when Andrew had insisted they went back to Whistler, refusing Saint's offer to join his pride.

He searched for something to say, his thoughts twisting and tangling, that knot in his chest pulling tight again.

Rune sighed. "I'm not happy about what she did, but imagine how it's been making her feel. I know Winnie… We both do… This is probably destroying her."

Maverick knew it was. He could feel it in her even at this distance. He could sense how carved up she was by what she had done, by how angry he was with her, and by the thought of her brother in the hands of the monsters at Archangel. Her shoulders shook as she cried and he looked away from her as she lifted her head and checked her arm. Guilt churned his stomach, had him avoiding looking at her and Rune. He had been rough with her, blinded by anger, and gods, if she hated him now, he deserved it.

Saint returned with an open laptop in his hands. "You might want to see this."

His alpha turned the device towards him and Rune and pressed a button, and Maverick forced himself to watch the video, to listen to Winnie as she desperately tried to convince the hunters not to hurt her brother. The pain in her voice, her obvious distress, cut him up inside and had his gaze shifting back to her. He exchanged a look with Rune, deeply aware of what he needed to do.

"I'm coming with you," Rune said.

"If you're going, then I'm going too." Callie came up beside her mate, her amber eyes bright with a need to fight. When Rune gave her a black look, she smiled sheepishly. "I might have been listening in."

"You're not coming with us." Rune held his hand up when she went to protest. "It isn't that I think you're not strong enough… It's because I can't lose you. I can't risk you, Callie."

"Neither of you are coming." Maverick shook his head when Rune turned a scowl on him instead. "Someone needs to stay here at the Ridge. If she's right and Archangel can track her devices, then there's a chance they know where she is. They know where we are."

Saint growled at that. "No one is raiding my pride. I'll alert everyone, including the cougars, and if Archangel dare come here, they'll be coming to their deaths."

Maverick looked off to his left, to Bronwyn, the need to go to her too strong to deny now. Nerves had him pulling down deep breaths as he walked away from the others, heading for her. If she lashed out at him, he wouldn't try to stop her from hitting him. He deserved her wrath. And if she hated him now, he deserved that too. He still couldn't believe that she loved him. Had loved him anyway. Before he had shown her what a monster he was.

She lifted her head as he neared her and looked at him. He cursed himself as he saw the fear in her reddened eyes, saw the hurt he had caused her, and looked at her arm. The bruise on it was already dark, clearly marking where he had gripped her too tightly. She looked there too, skimmed her hand over it and pulled the sleeve of her purple sweater down, covering it as she sighed.

He halted near her and willed her to look at him, but she kept her eyes firmly locked on the pebbles.

Maverick swallowed hard and wrestled with himself, trying to find the right words to say to make everything better, even when part of him felt nothing he could say would be adequate to make her forgive him. He heaved a sigh when nothing came to him and sat beside her instead, bent his knees and rested his forearms on them.

Stared at the water. And then at her.

She glanced at him, the fear gone from her eyes, but the hurt lingered.

"I'll help you," he husked, holding her gaze. "We'll get your brother back."

Her face softened, a light entering her honey-coloured irises as she looked at him, pushing out the hurt. He looked away from her, because he didn't deserve that look. She was looking at him as if he was a saviour again, when he had proven himself a monster. She knew him now. There was no more hiding things from her. She knew the kind of male he was, the things he was capable of, and she would distance herself.

And he couldn't blame her.

He stiffened as she pitched towards him and leaned her head against his bare arm, her hair soft and teasing his skin as her warmth seeped into him.

"I'm sorry," she whispered. "I never wanted to hurt you."

His heart drummed a sickening rhythm against his chest as a feeling ran through him, one that felt impossible even when the evidence of it was right there before him.

She wasn't going to distance herself.

"Was any of the last few days a lie?" His voice sounded tight in his ears, strained as he waited impatiently to hear the answer to that question.

She gave a small shake of her head, rubbing against his arm. "No."

He felt her nerves. Or was that his nerves?

"When you… ah… kissed me…" He couldn't bring himself to say anything more than that.

She lifted her head and gazed up at him, her eyes soft and warm, filled with affection and a hint of fear.

Did she really love him?

There was one way of finding out.

He cupped her nape.

Pulled her to him.

And kissed her.

CHAPTER 12

Bronwyn was spinning as Maverick kissed her, unable to keep up with what was happening. One moment it had looked as if he would never want to talk to her again and the next his mouth was on hers. She wasn't sure what to make of it. She wasn't sure what to make of him.

Part of her was angry with him for the way he had held her, bruising her, but the rest of her was angry at herself. He was right. She should have trusted him. She should have found a way to tell him what was happening rather than bottling it up, living in ridiculous fear of the hunters somehow discovering she had warned him. Maverick was strong, capable, and if anyone could find a way to help her without giving away that he knew what the hunters were up to, it was him.

Instead, she had lied to him and he had every right to be angry with her about it, to hate her for what she had done and what she had been planning to do.

He drew back just as she began kissing him, desperate to lose herself in it and put everything behind her, to forget their argument and that sense she had come close to destroying her chances with him.

His grey eyes dropped to her arm and the black slashes of his eyebrows furrowed as he stared at it, his gaze drilling into the spot where he had gripped her.

"I'm sorry," he whispered, his voice scraping low, filled with the hurt that shone in his eyes as he lifted them from her arm to lock with hers.

"I'm… I'm no good for you. I think I just proved that… showed you what a monster I am… and… I hate it."

He looked away from her and sighed, his broad bare shoulders heaving with it as he gazed off into the distance, an air about him that she didn't like. His thoughts were treading dark, despondent paths. It wasn't the first time he had been like this around her. Several times over the last few days he had withdrawn from her like this, bringing up an invisible barrier between them, and she knew why.

Maverick was struggling to see his worth, to believe he deserved a better life than the one he'd had back at the compound, where they had made him feel he was a beast, a male only good enough for the cages and entertaining others by spilling blood and taking punishing blows.

She looked at his hand as he placed it gently on her arm over the bruise, his profile still to her, a faraway look etched on his handsome face.

Bronwyn placed hers over it as she thought about what Rune had told her, held back a melancholy smile when Maverick tensed and glanced at her, a shocked edge to his eyes, one that told her he couldn't believe she would touch him like this after what he had done.

How little he thought of himself.

How had she failed to notice it before?

Maturing in the compound, in the arena, had done some serious psychological damage to Maverick, and that look in his eyes said he knew it. He knew what the cage had made him and he believed he would never overcome it.

She held his gaze, wishing he could see what she did. An honourable bear. A bear who had fought to protect her from the worst of the compound, had devoted himself to taking care of her even though she had been nothing to him. He'd had no reason to step in to protect her that day they had met. No reason to take her under his wing, to keep her safe for years. No reason to keep her out of the arena.

But he had done it.

Because beneath that sometimes growly and dark exterior beat the heart of a good male.

He just couldn't see it.

He only saw his faults.

Bronwyn stroked her fingers over his and looked at his scarred knuckles, the evidence of all the fights he had been forced to participate in and had survived.

She whispered to his hand, “You’re a good male, Maverick.”

His hand tensed beneath hers and he tried to take it back, but she seized it, refusing to let him pull away from her because he needed to hear this.

“A good male wouldn’t hurt a female like I hurt you,” he growled.

“True. I can’t excuse your behaviour and I don’t want to… but if you asked for forgiveness, I would give it to you.” She locked gazes with him, hoping he could see she meant that. “If you promised not to do it again.”

His eyebrows knitted hard and he muttered, “If you really knew the sort of male I am, you wouldn’t ask me to make a promise I can’t keep.”

Bronwyn huffed.

“You know, I can understand why you’re so hard on yourself, but at the same time, it’s infuriating.” She tugged his hand closer to her and turned it as much as she could, stroked her fingers over a deep scar that cut across the fleshy part of his palm near his thumb. “Remember how you got this?”

He looked at it and shrugged.

“I remember,” she whispered, her mind rolling back the years to that night. “You got this because you took my place in the cage. You got this because the hunters pitted you against a hellcat as punishment for making demands… for protecting me. That bastard almost killed you, because of me.”

“Winnie, watch your mouth,” he growled.

She rolled her eyes, because this wasn’t the compound. She swore now. She was grown up, mature. She had thoughts and fantasies that would probably shock him if he knew about them. She wasn’t little freckled-face Winnie the Pooh anymore. It was time he saw that.

“He was a bastard. The hunters were bastards too. They made you fight a shifter far stronger than you and then they beat you up afterwards. I know what happened, Maverick. I know what they did. You tried to hide it from me, but I know everything that went down that night.” Tears lined her lashes again as she thought about how messed up he had been, cut up and bleeding badly, and so agitated that he hadn't been able to keep still while she and Rune had been trying to tend to his wounds. She swallowed thickly. "You don't see it, but you're a good male. The hunters tried to kill that side of you, did terrible things to you and put you into fights while you were maturing, and it messed you up to a degree. I'm not going to deny that. It shaped you into a fighter—a survivor. They could have done that to me too, or I might have been passed from male to male as some of the other females were, too young to defend myself and too innocent to— You protected me from that, Maverick. A monster wouldn't have done that."

"I am a monster." He looked away from her but didn't try to take his hand away this time.

She sighed.

He pulled the sleeve of her sweater back and stared her hard in the eye. "Look at what I did and then look me in the eye and tell me I'm not a monster."

Bronwyn looked at her arm, at the handprint-shaped bruise on it that was dark against her skin and still ached a little, and knew she shouldn't be so fast to forgive him for what he had done, that she shouldn't make excuses for his behaviour, but deep in her heart she knew why he had lashed out at her.

She had hurt him. Not physically, but emotionally. She had betrayed him and it had wounded him, and he had thought everything she had done had been an act—including kissing him. He felt something for her and he felt she had used that against him, that her kiss had been a lie meant to lure him under her spell and into a trap.

It hadn't been.

It had been real.

On a deep sigh, she lifted her head and looked him in the eye, searched their clear grey depths and saw the hurt she had caused him, hidden beyond a barrier she wanted to break down. He was trying to keep his distance, his trust shaken by what she had done to him, and she could understand his need to hold the part of himself he had been slowly revealing to her over the last few days away from her now.

But there in his eyes, she found a glimmer of hope for her.

She had wounded him, had probably put a crack in his heart as she had with her own one, but just as she was willing to forgive him for what he had done, he wanted to forgive her. He wanted to believe what she was telling him.

He just didn't know how to do that. He didn't know how to handle the things she was making him feel. His time in the compound had affected him far more than she had ever imagined. Maverick was struggling to adjust to this world. He didn't know how to deal with his feelings, was caught up in a vicious cycle of believing himself a terrible person, that he was only good for one thing—fighting. The hunters must have drilled it into his head so deeply that he couldn't shake it. He honestly believed he was a bad person, no good for her, and no good for this world.

A male made for killing.

For violence.

All Bronwyn saw was a male who didn't know how to be soft, who had never been shown how to be careful or how to deal with his feelings.

He knew only the darker side of his instincts, of this world, gave in to them too easily because it was what had been expected of him. The compound had been no place for softness, for tender emotions. She had witnessed that for herself. The fighters had been hardened, taught through repeated violence to be just as violent and unforgiving themselves, had all of their softer feelings ripped away from them by the hunters and the cage.

Maverick had matured in that world.

For decades, he had been put through daily drills of the training ring, fights over perceived territory within the compound's free-roam areas, and battles to the death in the cage.

And then he had spent an equal amount of time trying to overcome all of that, to adjust to this world where he wasn't expected to be spilling blood and killing on an almost-daily basis, a world where the people around him weren't his enemy, liable to jump him at any moment to deliver a blow that would weaken him ahead of the next fight.

"I don't see a monster," she whispered, holding his gaze. "I only see a male who is trying his hardest to overcome a terrible past… one that shaped him into something he doesn't want to be. I only see a male who was never allowed to be soft and who fears that if he lets himself feel such emotions, he'll be punished."

She lifted her free hand and cupped his cheek, keeping his eyes on hers, aware that he would look away if she didn't make him look at her.

"I see a male who is afraid he doesn't know how to be gentle." She raised her other hand when he did try to avert his gaze, framed his face and made him look at her as her heart broke for him. "I see a male I want to help overcome those fears."

He wrenched away from her. "Because you pity me."

"No," she bit out and seized him by his nape, forcing him to look at her again. She gentled her grip when his eyes leaped to lock with hers. "Because I'm crazy about you, Maverick. Rune is right. It's always been you."

She gasped as he leaned towards her and captured her lips, as he kissed her. Hard at first, but he gentled it as she began to kiss him back, as she poured her feelings into it to show him that she wasn't afraid of him and that he didn't need to be afraid either. She was just getting into it again when he drew back and pressed his forehead to hers.

And breathed against her lips.

"Can we take this slow?"

She nodded, her heart going out to him again as she sensed his nerves. It wasn't difficult to agree to taking things slow with him when she wanted to savour this moment, this transition from her old life into one she had dreamed of for so long. She wanted this to last.

To be forever.

Rushing Maverick was a sure-fire way of ruining that.

Bronwyn stoked her courage and claimed his lips again, shivered at the softness of them as he brushed them over hers, their breaths mingling as he kissed her slowly. Tenderly. This was enough for her. This kiss. Being close to him like this.

Apparently, it wasn't quite enough for him, because he pulled away from her and stood.

When he held his hand out to her, her gaze leaped to his face, the soft but nervous look in his eyes hitting her hard and making her nervous too.

She slipped her hand into his and let him pull her onto her feet, and squeaked when he scooped her up into his arms. She looped hers around his neck and looked at him, into eyes that held a hint of affection now and made her want to stare into them forever.

He glanced towards the cabins on this side of the creek and she looked there too, and realised why he had stopped kissing her. Everyone had gathered there to stare at them. She didn't want an audience either, so she didn't complain when he carried her across the creek, preventing her from getting wet.

Maverick set her down when they reached the other side of it and she tried to act all business when she walked ahead of him towards the cabin, but the feel of him trailing behind her, his eyes drifting over her, from her head to her ass, made it hard. She wasn't sure why she was pretending they weren't going to the cabin to pick up where they had left off, putting on a show for Rune and the others. It wasn't going to fool anyone. Everyone had seen them kissing.

Everyone probably knew where this was going.

What was going to happen when they were alone in the cabin.

She blew out her breath, suddenly nervous as hell, and feeling awkward at the thought of Rune knowing she was doing her damnedest to get together with Maverick at last. A cursory glance over her shoulder in Rune's direction had her grimacing. He didn't look very happy about it as he watched Maverick like a hawk.

Like a father watching some male luring his daughter away to do wicked things to her.

Maverick was going to get a talking to later.

If he was aware of it, it didn't show on his face. His grey eyes were locked firmly on her nape, heat blazing in them that had another shiver traipsing down her spine as that spot tingled with awareness of his gaze upon it.

When she reached the steps up to the deck, his gaze lifted to her face, the hunger building in his eyes and heating her blood. She ached to have his lips on hers again, couldn't concentrate as she stared at his mouth.

And snagged her foot on the top step and almost fell flat on her face.

Maverick caught her around her waist, stopping her from falling.

Making her hyper-aware of his chest where it pressed against her back and how close he was to her. He loosed a low growl as he twisted her in his arms and kissed her again. His arms tightened around her, the show of strength sending an electric thrill through her that stoked a need to press her hands against him and fight him a little. She leashed that need, determined not to push him too hard. If she let her primal instinct to goad him into dominating her take the lead, she wasn't sure what would happen, but she knew Maverick wouldn't be happy with the outcome.

He was trying to be gentle.

His primal instincts were probably roaring at him to do the opposite. Like hers, his were no doubt pushing him to dominate her, to bend her to his will. She broke the kiss and brushed her hands over the flat slabs of his pectorals as she gazed up into his eyes, seeing the war playing out in them.

"We'll take this slow," she whispered and dropped her hand to his, caught hold of it and turned away from him to lead him into the cabin for a serious make-out session on the couch.

Kissing only.

Bronwyn tensed and froze as her phone jingled.

Her gaze lifted to the loft bedroom where she had left it.

Her heart pounded.

"You think it's them?" Maverick growled, and she wasn't sure whether he was unhappy about the interruption or the fact the hunters were contacting her again.

She swallowed hard and nodded.

Couldn't convince herself to go and check it because she knew what it would be—the location where she was supposed to take Maverick and Rune.

"I can't do this," she murmured and her heart hurt, whispering to her that if she didn't, Andrew was as good as dead.

"You can do this." Maverick took the lead, tugging her into the cabin, and settled her on the couch.

He crouched in front of her, the softness gone from his face, his expression hard and unyielding and his eyes cold and fierce.

"We're doing this. You and me. Together." A flicker of warmth entered his eyes as he growled those words, as he held her gaze and stroked her cheek. "Nothing bad is going to happen to you. I won't let them get their hands on you. I'll keep you safe."

"I'm not worried about me."

His handsome face softened and a hint of disbelief shone in his eyes.

He smiled tightly.

"You don't have to worry about me, Bronwyn."

He could say that, but it wouldn't stop her from feeling that way. It wouldn't stop her from thinking about how badly things could go, or how dangerous this was and that she might lose him.

He lifted his hand and smoothed his palm across her cheek, his eyes locked with hers.

"I can handle the hunters. I can handle whatever happens. I never really had a reason to fight before, but I do now."

He leaned in, bringing his lips close to hers.

And stole her heart.

"I'm going to fight for you… and the forever I want with you."

CHAPTER 13

Bronwyn pulled her car into a space overlooking Ghost Lake, butterflies fluttering in her stomach as she stared out at the dark water. Maverick placed his hand on her thigh as she clutched the steering wheel, battling the desire to put the car back into gear and get the hell away from the meeting place.

She had the feeling something terrible was going to happen, couldn't shake it as she glanced at Maverick and tried to breathe through her nerves. The corners of his lips twitched, as close to a smile as he had gotten since they had set off from the car park of The Spirit Moose after swapping his truck for her smaller hatchback.

"Everything will be fine, Winnie," he murmured and she nodded, but she didn't feel it.

When his hand slipped from her knee and he turned away from her, she wanted to grab him and tell him not to open the door. He was out of it before she could move and she followed suit, opening the driver's door and easing from the vehicle. Her gaze scanned the dark lot, butterflies becoming a hurricane as her senses stretched around her.

Nothing.

There wasn't a soul for as far as her acute senses could reach.

Maverick rounded the car to her, his face a black mask as he slipped into his role.

"Why did you bring me out here, Winnie?" he snarled and she tensed, reminded herself it was just an act and that they had to make this look good. He needed to look like he wasn't in on things or the hunters would grow suspicious.

Not that there were any nearby.

She stilled and stared at Maverick. Unless he could sense further than she could and had detected danger.

"It's just a stop off before we continue. I wanted to stretch my legs." That sounded lame even to her but at least she sounded flustered.

He folded his arms across his chest, causing his black cable-knit sweater to stretch tight over his biceps.

Distracting her.

Her bear side growled in approval of his visible strength, had her growing restless again. Kissing him had only made it harder for her to concentrate when she was around him. She kept thinking about how good his body had felt against hers, how firm and dominating his kiss had been, but also how tender it had been.

His eyes narrowed on her and he inhaled, growled as his jaw flexed and his gaze seared her.

A thrill chased through her, lighting up her blood, rousing that ache again—an ache only he could satisfy.

Maverick took a hard step towards her and she shivered at the thought he might grab her and kiss her, but instead he hissed, "Dial it back, Bronwyn. I can't focus for shit when you're looking at me like that."

She tried to tamp down her desire, wrangled her body back under control and squared up to him. "I told you, we need to get to Calgary. That's where he's waiting."

It was a risk to talk about a third party, but one Maverick had decided would be worth it. She had needed a reason for bringing him so far from his pride and the mountains, into the plains, and he had come up with needing his help with someone they had known in the compound.

"I should have had Rune come too. He'll want a piece of that bastard. Klaus deserves to die for what he did to Grace." Maverick prowled away from her, his agitation not an act.

She knew all about Grace and what had happened to her, how Rune had been forced to fight a polar bear called Klaus. Rune had failed to defeat him and so the hunters had made Grace take his place against the enormous male. She hadn't stood a chance.

Bronwyn tried to remember her next line.

Grunted as something hit her in her right shoulder, knocking it back, and cold spread outwards from that point.

She looked down at the dart protruding from her shoulder.

And then at Maverick.

"Run!" she screamed.

It was too late.

Maverick was already lunging for her as her legs gave out, trying to catch her, worry shining in his grey eyes. He growled as a dart hit him in his right thigh and went down hard, colliding with her and taking her down with him, landing on top of her.

Out cold.

Bronwyn fought the haze rolling over her, pushed free of Maverick's dead weight and growled as six men dressed in black combat gear came at her from all directions, the red lasers attached to their guns flashing in the darkness as they closed in on her.

She staggered to her feet, snarling and baring fangs at them, a powerful need to protect Maverick at the helm.

Pain burst outwards from the point of impact again as she ripped the dart from her flesh, as she cast it aside and growled at the men. They wobbled in her vision as it tunnelled and she shook her head, fighting to remain awake. Whatever dose they had hit her with, it hadn't been enough. They had known exactly what to hit Maverick with though. Because they had tranquilised him in the past, back at the compound? They had never hit her with a tranquiliser, must have guessed wrong about how much they would need to knock her out.

Their mistake.

She kicked her shoes off as black fur rippled over her skin, as she surrendered to the urge to shift and the dark hunger to rip these men apart to protect Maverick. A growl pealed from her as she tore at her clothes, shedding them, and shifted.

The moment all four paws hit the asphalt, she was running at the closest male.

"Contain her," one of the men barked.

Bronwyn felt the bite of another dart in her rump, kept running at the male but her actions grew sluggish, her steps faltering as cold swept through her and the edges of her vision darkened. She stumbled sideways as she neared the human and fell into a heap just inches from him.

Darkness swallowed her.

Voices wobbled in her ears, rolling back and forth in time with a black wave. Each time that wave receded, everything grew a little clearer, a little lighter. She frowned as her head ached, moaned as she felt the cold press of a hard floor against her side.

Her senses were slow to come back online, but when they did, they immediately blared a warning at her. Her heart lurched into her throat as she shot up into a sitting position, and she groaned as her skull felt as if it was ripping apart.

She pressed her hand to her head and leaned forwards.

"Winnie?" Maverick's voice warbled and she tried to focus on it, on him.

"I have to admit, I didn't expect you to be so effective," a man said.

Shock rolled through her.

She lifted her head and opened her eyes, couldn't believe what she was seeing as she stared through the thick steel bars at the owner of that voice.

"Andrew?" she breathed, struggling to grasp what was happening. "They let you go."

Relief flooded her and she smiled. It faltered when Maverick spoke.

"He was never their captive, Winnie."

She glanced at Maverick where he knelt in the cell next to hers, his hands resting on his jeans-clad knees.

Numbness swept through her as she looked at Andrew, into golden eyes that held not even a trace of warmth as he stared at her.

"What's he talking about?" She shuffled onto her knees and glanced down at herself as she realised she was wearing a black robe. She frowned as she remembered the hunters and shifting into her bear form to protect

Maverick, and then looked at her brother as she gathered the robe closed and tightened the belt. "Andrew? What's he talking about?"

Bronwyn looked him over, cold skating down her spine as she took him in and saw he was dressed in standard issue Archangel fatigues. She shook her head, unable to believe he was with them even as all the evidence she needed was right in front of her.

Movement off to her left caught her eye, dragging her focus away from Andrew. She could only stare as the female she had seen on the video call stepped into the corridor between the rows of cells and strode towards her brother.

"Preparations are being made to retrieve the other asset." The female slowed to a stop beside her brother and slid him a look. "Bringing only Maverick in wasn't our deal."

"I know. I'm as disappointed as you are. I really thought she could do it." He turned to the huntress. "But she played her part beautifully in a way. Drove her car as predicted. You were right to place a tracker on it."

Bronwyn gaped at her brother. "You put a tracker on my car?"

Gods, she had been such an idiot. She had been worrying about bringing her phone and laptop to Black Ridge, and they had been tracking her car.

"I should toss her in the arena just for making me wait in that backwater dump of a town until we could finally get a fix on her." The huntress buffed her nails and scowled down at Bronwyn.

Bronwyn glared right back at her, but it was Maverick who growled. Before he could say anything, Andrew continued.

"Sure, you had to wait, but now we have the location of a number of assets. If one of them is the bear who offered us a place in his pride, then we have nothing to worry about. With Rune and Maverick, and that alpha bear, we're off to a good start."

"A good start?" Bronwyn murmured, her brow furrowing as she looked up at her brother, her mouth drying out and heart picking up pace. "What are you talking about, Andrew?"

She didn't want to believe he was talking about what she thought he was, that he had done the unthinkable.

When he didn't respond, she pushed to her feet and stumbled to the bars, falling to her knees near them. She reached through the gap and seized the left leg of his black pants as she growled.

"Answer me."

Andrew slowly shifted his golden eyes to her hand and then eased to a crouch before her, pulling something from his pocket at the same time. He opened the heart locket and looked at it, his eyes darkening as he stared at the pictures it contained.

"Funny that she kept my picture in her locket. Just another attempt to make things look normal. Another lie." His eyebrows knitted hard as the corners of his mouth turned downwards. "I'm surprised she never replaced me with you… like she did in real life. You know… they always loved you more… but I suppose I can understand that. Who would love a bastard child like me?"

She gasped as she leaned back, her eyes widening.

He smiled coldly. "You didn't know. Don't be upset. No one was supposed to know. I was Dad's dirty little secret. A bastard offspring. The result of a drunken one-night stand with a female in Whistler. A human female."

"That's not—"

"Possible? Oh, I assure you it is. Our father was a no-good cheating asshole. When he found out about it, he confessed the ugly truth to our mother. To protect me and our shambles of a family, Mom agreed to move to another pride. They picked me up along the way and passed me off as their kid." Andrew snapped the locket closed, the suddenness of his actions making her jump as she struggled to take in what he was saying, as her whole life felt as if it was falling apart around her. "Mom always looked at me as if I was dirt. As if she despised me. Dad loved me at first, but after a while I could tell he was sick of the sight of me. I was a constant reminder of what he had done. Dad kept his promise and changed for the better, transforming himself into the perfect mate, and then you came along. Gods, they loved you. Both of them. And it sickened me. It sickened me to be near you, knowing how much they loved you, seeing them dote on you when all they felt for me was scorn."

"That's not true. They loved you." She tightened her grip on his trousers.

He huffed and grabbed her wrist in a bruising grip, twisted it as he glared at her. "When they died, I was glad. I was glad they were gone. I thought it was over. I was free. I thought I could build a life for myself, free of the stain of being a bastard, could make the pride see my worth. But then we were shipped off to our aunt and I knew the moment she looked at me that she knew… she knew I was nothing to her. She knew I was a bastard child, a weak bear."

Tears burned the backs of her eyes as she stared at Andrew, as she remembered how he had kept his distance from everyone at the pride, and how he had been distancing himself from her since he had matured.

"Did you ever love me?" she whispered, not wanting to know the answer to that question, but needing to ask it.

He cast her arm away from him. "No. Maybe. At times, I loved you. When our parents died and you looked at me as if I was your whole world. I tried to tell myself we were half-siblings, that we shared a father, and that meant something. It did for a while, but then the raid happened."

It struck her that he had changed when they had been brought to the compound because he had feared if he shifted and attempted to protect her, the other bear shifters would know he was born of weak stock, the product of a mating between a human and a bear. If his mother had been their father's fated one and bound to him, he would have been as strong as him. That bond would have increased his mother's strength and healing, and increased her lifespan to that of their father.

But she had been some run of the mill human.

He slid Maverick a black look, his golden eyes narrowing. "You swept in to save my sister and the way she looked at you… at Rune. Gods, I hated her."

Bronwyn flinched. "Brother…"

"Don't *brother* me. You treated them better than you had ever treated me. You loved them more than you had ever loved me," he barked and she flinched away again. That wasn't true, and deep in his heart he had to know it. He had to. He glared at her and then Maverick. "You were so strong. The glorious prized fighters. I knew I wouldn't stand a chance against you in a fight… that there was no way for me to win my sister back."

Maverick growled. "So you abandoned her. If you had come to us, we would have protected you too."

Andrew scoffed. "Protection? I didn't need or want your protection. I would never submit myself to something so abhorrent to me. I found another way to protect myself. Your betrayal allowed me to wash my hands of you and focus on building a better life for myself."

"My betrayal?" She felt those words as a blade in her heart. Her brother had lost his mind. Was he really so jaded by life that he viewed what she had done as an act of betrayal? She shook her head. "Maverick and Rune offered me protection. If I hadn't taken it, gods know what would have happened to me, Andrew."

He scowled down at her. "Because the gods know I wasn't strong enough to protect you. That's what you're saying, isn't it, dear sister? I wasn't strong enough to keep you safe, so you traded up. You played the damsel in distress to get the two best fighters to take you into their protection. I bet you fucked them every night to keep them on your side too."

"Watch your mouth," Maverick snarled and looked ready to launch at her brother.

"Or what? The cage is reinforced steel. I admit, it's not the high-tech facility we were held in before, but the budget didn't allow for it. We only have a couple of modern cells and one of those is occupied. Maybe after the money begins rolling in, we can upgrade the rest of the accommodation. Although, I'll enjoy keeping you in a cage like this, like the animal you are. I know all about your exploits, bear. Better watch *your* mouth." Andrew smiled coldly when Maverick reared back as if he had been struck, his handsome face darkening as her brother issued that threat.

What did he know about Maverick that was enough to have him turning so submissive? Looking so afraid as he glanced at her?

"Where was I? Oh, yes. I learned quickly to gain the favour of the hunters. It was important to my survival. I made some alliances that continued long after we were freed." He looked up at the huntress. "Sylvia here, for example. Her father used to run the compound where we were held. Imagine my surprise when she cornered me in Vancouver close to seven years ago and offered me a deal."

"A deal?" Bronwyn felt sick as it hit her. "Those trips. Every time you went to Vancouver… you were…"

She couldn't bring herself to say it.

Maverick snarled, "He's been supplying the hunters with the locations of prides, working with the enemy."

Bronwyn pressed her hand to her stomach. "Gods, Andrew. Why?"

He rose to his feet and looked at Sylvia, and the answer hit her. He had embraced the human part of his blood, because of the female. She had seduced him into a different form of slavery, capturing his heart, turning him to their side.

"It's a lucrative business. It was all going well. I had enough money for a penthouse overlooking Stanley Park, had a woman warming my bed, and wanted for nothing. Until someone at Archangel discovered the arena and closed it down." Andrew reached out and brushed his knuckles across the female's cheek, his golden eyes warming. "Sylvia had the idea to make a new arena, one serving hunters stationed in and around Calgary. Vancouver HQ is focused on their local area. A compound out in the sticks isn't even going to register on their radar. Of course, we needed big names to draw the crowds."

"So you sent me to Rune and Maverick." She couldn't believe her own brother was behind everything and had betrayed her. Her brow furrowed as she looked up at him, her heart breaking. "I thought you were in danger. I was afraid they were going to kill you. I've spent the last few days terrified. That hunter had a knife to your throat."

"I had to make it look convincing." He slid a black look at Maverick. "I know how much you love these bears… your *protectors*. You were so quick to steal Winnie from me. I hated you for that."

"What you hated was the fact I was stronger than you," Maverick spat and rolled his shoulders. "How about we meet in the cage and see which of us walks out of there alive? My money is on me."

Andrew chuckled. "You'll be going in the cage, but it won't be me you'll be fighting."

"No," she bit out and reached for her brother again, but he moved back a step, evading her. She threw a wild look up at him. "Please, Andrew. Don't do this."

He scoffed. "What did you think would happen if you brought him to me? Are you so naïve that you honestly thought I wanted him for a reason other than his prowess in the arena?"

No, she wasn't, but part of her had begun to believe it wouldn't come to this. She looked at Maverick, hating herself for what she had done, and that it was for nothing. Andrew had betrayed her and now Maverick was going to be forced to fight again. Her heart felt close to breaking as she gazed at him, as she thought about what her brother had done.

Andrew moved closer to her again, recapturing her attention. "You know… you could have been on this side of the bars if you hadn't chosen to betray me. It took a lot of effort to get Maverick's number. The huntress we sent to seduce him when we located him in Vancouver this winter had her work cut out getting him to hand over his digits, but it was worth it."

Bronwyn couldn't hold back the growl that erupted from her as she thought about Maverick with another female.

Maverick was quick to reach for the bars that separated them, his tone soft as he said, "Don't let him poison your mind, Winnie. I never slept with that female. I should have known the bitch was up to something, coming up to me in that bar each night, flirting with me no matter how many times I told her I wasn't interested. Must have been a week of her hounding me before she snatched my phone and swapped our details before I could get it back off her."

She looked from him to Andrew. "If you had his number, why involve me?"

"It was a test." Andrew's eyes remained cold and unreadable as he stared down at her.

"It was sick," Maverick snarled.

Andrew slid him a look. "I admit, Sylvia wanted to track you via your phone to your pride, even went against my wishes and tried it, but you dropped off the radar and we lost you. That's when I came up with a plan. You would do anything for my sister, and if I got her to call you, she would undoubtedly lead me straight to you. We needed to get the new facility up and running first. The moment it was ready for you and Rune, I staged my capture and set the ball rolling on bringing you in."

When his gaze shifted back to her and darkened, Bronwyn tensed.

"And you failed the test."

She shook her head, a weak denial that did nothing to ease the guilt slowly building inside her. "You're wrong. We came to save you. I didn't tell Maverick anything. He overheard me talking to Sylvia and I had to tell him you'd been taken captive. He offered to help me rescue you."

"You picked him over me," Andrew growled, flashing fangs. "You'll always pick him over me."

She reached for him again as tears burned her eyes, a desperate need to make him see that she hadn't betrayed him sweeping through her, to make him see that she loved him, but he evaded her.

"We'll make it interesting. A big opening night fight to draw the crowds." Andrew moved to stand in front of Maverick's cell. "An old friend of yours was more than happy to return to the fold in exchange for the chance to bloody his fists and fangs again. If you can defeat Klaus, then my sister goes free. If you fail, then she'll be next to fight him and you'll have to watch."

"You son of a bitch. She's your sister! How the hell can you do this to her?" Maverick launched at the bars, slamming into them as he reached an arm between them. He growled as Andrew took two steps back, placing himself beyond Maverick's reach. "Let her go. I'll fight if you let her go."

Bronwyn shook her head and pushed to her feet, moved to the bars that separated her and Maverick and gripped them. "No. You can't fight him. No."

The polar bear would kill him.

"Neither of you get a say in the matter. Maverick fights Klaus, and if he fails to beat him, you're next in the cage." Andrew swept away from them, Sylvia following close on his heels.

Bronwyn sagged to her knees, all her strength leaving her. She couldn't believe her own brother would do such a thing to her, to Maverick. She wanted to bury her head in her knees and hide there, some part of her desperate to believe this was all a nightmare brought on by the tranquiliser and that she would wake up to find both she and Maverick were safe.

Maverick came to her and placed his hands over hers, gently eased them away from the bars and held them.

She stared at him, heart aching as fear and anger collided inside her, despair mingling with them to make her feel as if she was being torn apart. Her gaze fell to the thick metal collar around his neck, one designed to prevent him from shifting, to keep him in line. All it would take was a press of a button and he would be drugged, knocked out and left vulnerable. She had done that to him. She had put that collar back on him, one he had always hated, one they had never bothered to place on the weaker females like her. She should be wearing that collar, not him. He didn't deserve this. This was all her fault.

"I'm sorry," she whispered, despair quick to fill her, together with self-loathing.

The black slashes of his eyebrows furrowed and he shifted his left hand to her face, cupping her cheek as he stroked his thumb over it. "Hey now. It's fine. Everything is going to be fine."

His grey eyes softened.

"I'll keep my promise, Bronwyn. Nothing is going to happen to you. Nothing is going to happen to me. I'll win this fight."

She wished she could believe him.

The ache in her chest worsened as she thought about him being locked in the cage with that polar bear, forced to face the same terrible trial as Rune. Rune had failed and Grace had paid the ultimate price.

And Bronwyn feared that was about to happen to her.

CHAPTER 14

Maverick tried to tamp down the fear and contain the rush of adrenaline that the thought of facing Klaus in the cage had running through him. He brushed his palm across Winnie's cheek, focusing on her, surrendering to his need to take care of her. Her brother had dealt her a serious blow, one that was going to have a lasting effect on her. It was going to take her a long time to overcome what Andrew had done, but Maverick would be there for her every single second of every single day.

Presuming he survived the cage.

He stared at her, determination building inside him as she gazed at him, fear and affection in her honey-coloured eyes.

And hope.

He wouldn't fail her. He would best the bear who had killed Grace and he would free Bronwyn, even if it killed him. He wouldn't let her go through what Grace had. He wasn't sure how he was going to free her, but he would find a way.

First, he had to kill Klaus.

Defeating him wasn't enough.

The polar bear had to die. It was what Rune would want and it was what Maverick would do for his friend.

Fear for Rune and his other friends at Black Ridge was swift to run through him as he thought about what the huntress had said. They were preparing to go there to capture the rest of his pride. He couldn't let that happen either.

Somehow, he needed to win this fight, save Bronwyn and escape this hell, and then save his pride.

One step at a time.

He ached when Bronwyn leaned into his touch, her eyes slipping closed, causing tears to tumble down her cheeks. Her pain echoed inside him and he wasn't sure what to say. He didn't know how to take her pain away. It wasn't just what Andrew had done causing her hurt. It was what she had done.

He stroked her face and murmured, "Don't blame yourself. I knew what I was getting into when I decided to help you. We'll get out of this."

Her eyes opened and locked with his, the flicker of hope in them slowly fading.

So he smiled for her.

Lined up all the things he wanted to tell her, things he knew would make her feel better and give her hope, a reason to keep looking to the future and believing in him.

"Up," someone growled, and Maverick jerked and twitched as a burst of electricity hit the back of his neck thanks to his collar.

He swung a black look at the dark-haired hunter standing at the door of his cell.

The male waggled the device he held. "Up or the next blast will be enough to fry her brain too."

Maverick snarled but lumbered onto his feet, shaking off the effects of being hit with a few thousand volts. His hand slipped from Winnie's face and he looked down at her, wishing he had more time.

"Move it." The hunter unlocked the cage and Maverick flashed fangs at him, warning the male to back off and give him a second.

He had to tell Winnie something.

The hunter hit the button again, sending another few thousand volts shooting down Maverick's spine and spiderwebbing over his skull. Bronwyn launched to her feet, snarling through her fangs at the hunter as her eyes flashed with fire. The anger in her eyes turned to fear as she shifted her gaze to him, her brow furrowing as she clung to the bars that separated them.

There was more than fear in those bewitching honey irises.

There was love too.

He stared at her, hoping she could see how deeply he loved her too.

Maverick backed away from her, heading for the cell door, holding her gaze until the last possible moment. The second he was clear of the door, the hunter shoved him in his back, forcing him away from her.

Giving him another reason to survive the coming fight.

He would tell her the things he had wanted to say then. He would tell her that she was his fated one and that he was in love with her, and that he would never regret anything about how they had come to be together. Not even this.

Maverick strode along the corridor between the rows of empty cells, his shoulders tipped back and head held high.

He breathed through the fear and the doubts, focused his mind as he followed the directions of the human behind him, keeping his gaze locked ahead of him as they navigated a maze of corridors. Always ahead of him. The fight lay there and if he didn't focus on it, didn't hone his mind and his body, preparing himself, he would lose it.

He couldn't lose this fight.

A door ahead of him buzzed and swung open, and he swallowed hard at the sight of the holding room. It resembled the one he used to find himself in every other night. Crisp white walls. Plain concrete floor. A table bolted to the middle of it.

A burn lit up his blood at the sight of that cold steel table.

"Get in and strip. You know the drill." The hunter shoved him in his back and Maverick growled at him, turned to strike the male but the door closed in his face.

He exhaled hard, trying to shake off the spike in aggression, calming his mind again. It was hard as he pivoted on his heel and found himself staring at the table, seeing flashes of females bared on one just like it, begging him for more.

Maverick closed his eyes and focused on Bronwyn. Would they bring her to the cage to watch the fight? There would be an observation room with a one-way mirror if they had set things up like the other arenas. Her brother would probably move her there, forcing her to watch him fight and keeping her on hand for him to shove into the cage if Maverick failed.

He wasn't going to fail.

He kept telling himself that as he stripped off his clothing, folded it neatly and set it on the end of the table. He grabbed the pair of plain black shorts someone had left for him, ones that were snug and reached to mid-thigh, and pulled them on. Gods, it was all so sickeningly familiar.

Maverick went to the other door in the room, one off to his right, and stood facing it. He breathed slowly, pulling air in through his nose as he stared at the steel panel, and went through the same stretches he had always completed before a match, limbering up as he mentally prepared himself.

Klaus was bigger than him, but slower. He could use that to his advantage.

He had seen the male fight too, had studied his moves even though he had known they wouldn't be pitted against each other. The hunters had preferred to keep their prized fighters away from each other. It hadn't stopped Maverick from studying every single male in the compound, putting to memory things like which foot or fist he favoured, and any tell they might have.

Maverick flexed his fingers and curled them into fists as he blew out his breath, still struggling to get his nerves under control. Rune hadn't been able to beat Klaus and that had been when he was at the height of his prowess in the cage. Maverick was sorely out of practice and he wasn't sure he was strong enough to best Klaus.

He shut down those thoughts, purging them from his mind. He could do this. He had to do this. If he didn't win, then Bronwyn would face the same fate Grace had.

His beautiful black bear wouldn't stand a chance.

She was at least four hundred pounds lighter than Klaus in her bear form, and a good two hundred pounds lighter in her human one, and she wasn't a fighter. All it would take was one well-aimed blow and Klaus would kill her.

Maverick pressed his palms to the door and leaned against it, breathed through the panic that tried to grip him as he thought about her in the cage. It wasn't going to happen. He was going to beat Klaus.

He set his jaw and stared at the door, his eyes narrowing as he repeated that in his head.

He was going to beat Klaus.

He was going to win.

The door buzzed and opened, and he caught himself before he tipped forwards with it. He growled and rolled his shoulders as he straightened his spine, as he tipped his head up and drew down a deep breath. His gaze locked on the narrow corridor ahead of him, one that was dark.

It carried the scent of humans. Lots of them.

On a feral snarl, Maverick stalked forwards into the gloom, each step he took cranking him tighter as the faint buzz of conversation and the scent of excitement coming from the crowd swirled around him. Adrenaline surged, made him twitch as he got swept up in the sounds and scents, in the thought of the arena that waited ahead of him. It all transported him back in time, had him feeling as if he had never left, as if his life in Black Ridge had been some dream and now he was awake.

Lights flashed across the end of the tunnel and the crowd grew more agitated, sending up whoops as the volume increased, and the scent of spilled beer and adrenaline fired him up.

He strode from the tunnel onto the raised floor of the twenty-foot-wide circular cage, scanned the room beyond the two rows of reinforced bars that contained him. It was dark, the lights turned low, but he could make out the hundred or so hunters lurking in the shadows at tables and a bar, all of their eyes on him.

Maverick roared at them, and relished the way they fell silent as fear spiked the scents in the air and then erupted into a cheer.

Gods, it was addictive.

Like coming home.

He shook that thought away and reminded himself that home was a long way from here, back at Black Ridge, and he needed to get back there. It was hard to deny the high of the cage though, the anticipation and excitement that collided with the fear in him, had him restless as he waited for the other door to open, his eyes fixed on it as the one behind him closed.

Spotlights swung towards it, leaving him and giving his sensitive eyes a reprieve that allowed him to see the room around the cage more clearly. As predicted, there was a one-way mirror in a wall off to his right, between the two tunnels that ran from the cage at an angle and would have formed a triangle with the wall had it not been for the circle of steel bars that intersected the point where the tunnels would have met.

Maverick moved to stand at that point, right in the centre of the hard floor someone had painted with a bullseye.

He glared at the door as it opened, at the seven-foot platinum blond male who had to stoop to exit it without banging his head.

Klaus straightened and raised his fists in the air.

"And the crowd goes wild," Maverick muttered as everyone cheered.

He backed off towards his door, raked a gaze over the male to assess him and spot any changes to his physique that might indicate a weakness.

The big bastard looked just as packed with muscle as he had been all those years ago.

Klaus grinned at him, flashing a missing fang, the scar on the right side of his jaw pulling tight. His Nordic accent was strong as he growled, "Still screwing that black bear?"

Maverick flipped him off. "If you get your kicks thinking about me and Rune going at it, then you do you… just keep it to yourself."

Klaus rolled thickly hewn shoulders and grunted, "Will be a shame to kill you."

"To the death then?" Maverick subtly flexed his fingers, anticipation curling through him as he waited for the go signal.

Klaus nodded.

Maverick's collar clicked open and he kicked off, leaving it to tumble to the floor as he launched at Klaus.

The polar bear's collar dropped away and he swung his right fist at Maverick. Maverick slid under it and twisted, threw a punch that nailed

Klaus in the back near his kidney. Klaus pivoted and grabbed Maverick, and hurled him.

He grunted as he hit the bars, the back of his head cracking off the cold steel, and snarled as the crowd jeered. He pushed off, launching back at Klaus, leaped right when the polar bear swung at him and came around behind him.

Maverick kicked him in the back of his knee and slammed his fist into the back of his head as he went down. The male grunted as he hit the deck and struggled to shake off the blow. Maverick grinned. Payback was a bitch.

He levelled a hard kick at Klaus's stomach and then another, forcing the bear onto his side. Klaus caught his foot when he made the mistake of going for a third kick and twisted it hard. Pain tore up his leg and he cried out as it felt as if his knee was about to dislocate. He twisted with it, stopping Klaus from hobbling him, and lost his balance.

Hit the floor.

Damn it.

He rolled before Klaus could pin him, narrowly evading the male, and came up on his feet on the other side of the cage. Klaus barrelled towards him, rage lighting his blue eyes, and white fur rippled over his bare skin. Maverick braced himself, even when he knew the male wouldn't shift. It was the unspoken rule of the ring.

Everyone who had come through the ranks in the arena had done so without resorting to using their animal forms, denying the hunters the thrill of seeing them shift.

Maverick took the hit, grunted as Klaus's shoulder struck him hard in his chest and his back slammed into the side of the cage with enough force to rattle the bars. He gripped the polar bear's shoulders and brought his knee up, striking him in the stomach, hitting him over and over again as Klaus punched him in his side. The coppery tang of blood flooded his mouth as he breathed and he shoved Klaus off him, breaking free of him before he could deal any more damage.

Klaus breathed hard as he backed away, his stomach reddened by Maverick's blows, and then rushed him again.

Maverick was ready for him, swept around to his right to evade him and leaped backwards, keeping the space between them steady. Klaus growled as he pivoted, turning on a pinhead, and stormed towards him. This time, Maverick charged him, the hunger to strike the male too strong to deny.

They collided hard, drawing another cheer from the crowd, one that was like a drug to Maverick. He craved that sweet high. The chanting of his name. The feel of his fist striking bone. The taste of blood on his tongue.

It hit him as hard as Klaus did, his fist slamming into Maverick's jaw to knock his head to one side. Rather than grunting in pain, he growled in pleasure. Gripped Klaus by his nape and headbutted him. Klaus recoiled and Maverick dragged his head down and brought his knee up, smashed it into his face and released him as he staggered backwards.

A dark veil descended, the need for violence swallowing him, making him forget everything else. There was only the high. It was everything he needed. Everything he craved. He took another hard hit and tried to counter, but Klaus saw it coming. The big polar bear hit him with a one-two punch, knocking his head side to side, rattling his brain in his skull, and a different sort of darkness encroached.

Panic surged through him, the thought that he might lose this fight a shot of adrenaline he badly needed as his body ached from the blows Klaus had delivered. He grappled with the male again, kicking and punching as best he could at such close quarters, growing aware that he wasn't strong enough to take him down as it stood. Klaus was tiring, but Maverick was tiring faster.

He grunted as Klaus threw him across the ring, as he crashed into the door to one of the tunnels and hit the floor. Blood burst from his lips, the acrid tang of it strong on his tongue, and he struggled for air as he tried to muster the strength to get up.

He had to turn the tables somehow or it was game over.

The crowd seemed to think it was already over, were chanting Klaus's name as the male stalked towards Maverick, a cold look in his eyes as he cracked his bloodied knuckles.

Maverick bared fangs at him.

It didn't end here.

Like this.

It couldn't.

Klaus slid a look at the one-way mirror, a cruel smile twisting his lips, a light entering his eyes. "I hear a little female is my next opponent. Maybe I'll treat her nicely… fuck her right here in the middle of the ring before I kill her."

The crowd cheered.

Maverick snapped.

He shot to his feet, snagging the open collar from the floor, and roared as he ran at Klaus.

The male turned his head to look at Maverick.

Too late.

Maverick smashed the end of the steel collar into the side of his head, wielding it like a weapon. Blood trickled down Klaus's temple as he pitched to his right and Maverick didn't give him a chance to recover. He snarled and bared fangs as he slammed the collar into his head again.

Klaus blocked his next blow, but it didn't stop Maverick. Rage stole control of him, the thought of this male treating Winnie like that ripping another vicious roar from him. Fur swept over his arms as he gripped the collar in both hands and swung hard, striking Klaus in the face with it. The male lost his footing and fell.

Maverick leaped on top of him, smashed the collar into his head over and over again, caught up in the anger that poured like hot acid through his veins, unable to deny his primal need to protect his fated female.

When his arms ached and shook too fiercely for him to keep going, he sagged and let the collar fall from his grip.

Stared at what he had done.

Blood covered the floor beneath Klaus's body, slowly spreading outwards.

The crowd remained deathly quiet.

Only the sound of his rough breaths reached his ears as he lumbered onto his feet, as he stumbled backwards, unable to believe what he had done. He had killed him.

He had killed Klaus.

Grace was avenged.

Winnie was safe.

Maverick threw his head back and roared.

The cheers of the crowd and the adrenaline of winning were like a high, transporting him back to all the times he had fought in the arena. He stared at the crowd, relishing their chants, their excitement. It was like a drug to him.

A drug he had been addicted to.

An addiction he thought he had shaken.

But it hooked him again in a heartbeat.

"Collar on," someone said over the PA system.

Excitement instantly flooded him, his aches forgotten as he reached for the bloodstained collar and his mind raced forwards. He easily obeyed, snapped the collar back in place as a different sort of hunger surged through him.

The door opened and he strode towards it, entered the tunnel and didn't slow his pace, his eyes locked on the door at the other end of it.

His skin felt too tight as his blood rushed, his body primed for a good, hard release, hungry for a soft female. As much as he tried to deny that darker part of himself he had courted in this underground world, he couldn't shake the fierce need that gripped him.

The door ahead of him opened and he stepped into the holding room.

When it closed behind him, the other door buzzed.

Maverick was laser-focused on it in a heartbeat, hunger swelling inside him, making him rock hard in an instant.

Only it was Bronwyn they pushed into the room.

Bronwyn wearing only that black robe.

The thought that she was bare beneath it inflamed him, had him growing harder, eager to toss her onto the table and take her.

He couldn't.

"Maverick!" She went to run to him, her eyes lighting up with relief he could sense in her together with concern as they catalogued his injuries.

Maverick growled at her and backed away when she stopped, drawing up short of him, a worried look crossing her face.

"Leave," he snarled, fear closing his throat, pounding inside him as fiercely as the hunger. "I can't be near you right now. I can't."

He would hurt her. He would show his true colours to her.

And she would never want to see him again.

She blinked.

"Leave!" he roared, barely holding himself back as the urge to sweep her into his arms grew stronger, pressing him to surrender to it. "Now!"

She tensed and backed off a step, fear flittering across her delicate features.

She looked over her shoulder at the door.

It slammed shut.

CHAPTER 15

Maverick stormed to the door and banged his fists against the featureless metal panel. “Let her out!”

Anger and frustration mingled with the fear running through his veins, amping it up and giving his needs a firmer grip on him. Bronwyn didn’t help matters.

She took a step towards him and softly whispered, “Maverick.”

He snarled and bashed the door, raining blows down on it that had the sides of his fists aching. When that didn’t work and the rage, the despair, got the better of him, he punched it. Flat out punched it as hard as he could. His knuckles burned with each blow, the sound of metal being struck echoing in his ears together with his own harsh breaths.

“Maverick, stop!”

Bronwyn took another step towards him, her desperation hitting him hard, together with her fear. She feared him. He pressed his palms to the door, his hands throbbing, and leaned forwards, not caring when his forehead struck the cold metal.

“Open the door. Don’t do this.” He sounded bleak even to his own ears, was deeply aware of her gaze on his bare back as he sagged against the door, his fight leaving him as despair swallowed him.

He didn’t want to hurt her. He didn’t want her to see that part of himself, a side he thought had died a long time ago, but it was still within him.

Still had control of him.

Just the scent of Bronwyn was enough to have him rock solid in his shorts, primed for a hard fuck. He pressed his forehead into the door and screwed his eyes shut, cursing the hunters for doing this.

Cursing her brother.

The bastard knew the sort of male Maverick was, must have witnessed it for himself after a fight. The hunters had never been subtle about watching them in the holding rooms. One wall of the security room had been thick toughened glass and the monitors had faced it, revealing everything to anyone passing by.

Maverick banged against the door again as his rage roared back to the fore, provoked by the thought her brother would subject her to this side of him, that he would do this to her when she loved him. Andrew had it all wrong, was caught up in some lie he had made himself believe, thought that Winnie didn't need him because he wasn't strong enough, that she had rejected him. He didn't deserve her love, but he had it.

"What's wrong?" she murmured and moved closer to him.

"Stay away from me," he growled and paced away from her, feeling like a caged animal.

He couldn't bring himself to look at her, not even to see the hurt that would be shining in her eyes. Hurt he had caused with his vicious words. He didn't want to push her away. He didn't want to hurt her.

But he had to.

It was for her own good.

Her scent was driving him crazy and awareness of her ran deep in his veins, rousing his blood and his primal instincts, pushing him to dominate her. Gods, he was so hard for her, and part of him knew it wasn't just because of the victory high or the fact he had trained his body to expect release after he had won in the cage. He wanted her so badly. And her brother and the hunters knew it. This was punishment, for both of them.

Andrew wanted him to attack her and take her, to treat her as he had all those other females in the past. Her brother wanted him to ruin things between them, and he wanted to hurt her, making her believe she had been wrong to turn her back on him. Andrew wanted to take everything from both of them and destroy them.

Maverick flicked a glare at the camera mounted in one corner of the room and roared at it.

"I'm getting out of this cell and I'm going to fucking murder you for doing this." He breathed hard, desperately trying to calm himself as he stared at the camera, but he couldn't. His body expected release, and the longer he left it, the worse it would get.

He had tried to deny himself pleasure before, had made the hunters take the female away, thinking he could overcome his addiction. In the end he had been a wreck, had been aching so hard for a fix that he had gotten into fights with everyone and had found himself in solitary. The hunters had brought another female to him, and he had been rougher than usual with her.

He couldn't be rough with Winnie.

He didn't want to be that male with her.

Maverick cursed himself this time. This was all his fault. He had courted this side of himself, had let himself grow used to this pattern, and now he couldn't shake it. Two decades and he fell back into his old ways in a heartbeat. What hope was there for him?

He wanted to be a gentle male for Winnie. He wanted to be a good male. Tonight had proven he didn't have a snowball's chance in Hell of making that happen. Rage turned to despair again, to hopelessness that pulled him down, had him storming to the camera and leaping for it. He growled as he ripped the damned thing from the wall, as he utterly destroyed it. Snarled as he pivoted and paced away from the wreckage.

Bronwyn's gaze tracked him. "What's wrong, Maverick?"

He turned on her, a little too sharply judging by how she tensed and plastered herself against the wall close to the door. He sighed and eased back a step, closed his eyes and hung his head.

"This is torture… I can't take it," he whispered. "Just… stay over there. Maybe I can get myself under control."

He wasn't sure that he could. In fact, he knew he couldn't, was only fooling himself by thinking this was going to end well. The dark urge to sink himself between her thighs was only growing stronger as the seconds trickled past at an agonisingly slow rate.

When her gaze dropped to his body and softened, worry filling her eyes, he stormed to the table and grabbed his jeans. He used them as a cloth, rubbing the blood away, not wanting her to see him like this, and aware that she would want to come to him and take care of him if he didn't clean up. He needed her to keep her distance.

He didn't feel the sting of the cuts or the ache of the bruises as he cleaned himself up, felt only the pounding need building inside him as he grew hyper-aware of her where she lingered near the door. Her scent swirled around him, tormenting him, worsening his need.

"Is this about what you used to do after fights?" Those softly spoken words rolled over him and knocked him off-balance all over again.

Maverick snapped his head up and stared at her as shock swept through him, making him cold to the bone.

His blood was like ice in his veins as he stared at her.

"You know about that?" He lowered his hand and his jeans fell from it as he struggled to believe she did.

She averted her gaze, a blush climbing her cheeks as she toyed with the cuff of her robe, and whispered, "I do."

Anger blazed up his blood, shame swift to follow it, making him feel dirty and tainted, and gods, she would never want him now. She knew the things he had done back then, when he had been fresh from a fight, high on the thrill of it. He really was no good for her.

"How do you know about it?" he snapped, not angry at her, angry at himself.

She lifted her head and stared at him, not a trace of fear in her honey-coloured eyes as they locked with his. "Because you tried to hide it from me?"

He had. He had never wanted her to know about what he did, had always made sure to avoid her until he had showered and calmed down. Usually, that had meant he didn't see her until the day after he had fought.

She held his gaze, looking bold and courageous, stirring his blood all over again. She had grown up beautiful and strong, but not strong enough to handle him. Beneath that façade of courage was the same gentle Winnie he had known back then, the same tender and caring female.

"You could stop me from seeing that side of you, but you couldn't stop some of the others from talking about it." She dropped her hands to her sides and bluntly said, "Rumours spread about you and I was curious. One night I was passing the security room and… I saw."

Sickness brewed in his stomach like hot acid, scouring his insides.

Bronwyn took a step towards him, determination flashing in her eyes.

Maverick held his hand up to stop her and backed off, trying to place more distance between them, some foolish part of him hoping it would be enough to allow him to rein in his dark desires.

But his bare back hit the wall.

No escape.

He flicked a desperate look at the door. "Open it! Let her go."

As expected, no one answered.

"They're not going to let us out until we—are they?" Bronwyn slid a look at the door and then him.

The fact that she couldn't bring herself to talk about screwing him compounded the feeling that she didn't want him, that she knew what a monster he was now and she was no longer interested in him. He tried to shake off the hurt, but it refused to go, whispered taunts in his mind and carved a hole in his heart.

She glanced at the broken camera. "They can't see us. Maybe we can pretend we had sex?"

Maverick countered, "I doubt that's the only camera in the room. It's the only one we can see."

He shook his head when she advanced a step.

"Don't." Control was a fragile thing for him and her scent was driving him crazy.

The urge to grab her and take her was strong, only with her it was different. He didn't just want to throw her on the table and spend himself inside her, using her to slake his hunger and give himself a fix.

He wanted to kiss her.

He wanted to savour her and do things right, even when he wasn't sure what right was or whether he was capable of it at that moment.

"I can't do this," he husked. "We can't do this."

Her brow furrowed, hurt flaring in her golden eyes now. "Because you don't want me?"

"Gods, no. I want you… more than you can know… and that's the reason I can't do this. I don't want to hurt you, Bronwyn." His shoulders slumped and he sagged back against the wall. "If you know the rumours, if you really saw me, then you know how rough I am with females. You know that I'm… not right. There's something seriously wrong with me."

And for one beautiful moment back at Black Ridge, he had thought he could overcome it, had been relieved by her promise they would take things slow, believing it was all he needed to change himself for the better.

She braved another step towards him. "There's no way out of this. Unless you plan for us to stay here until we both starve to death?"

Maverick didn't think he could last that long. The need beating inside him was only growing stronger and sooner or later, he was going to snap. Already, the clarity the sight of her had given him was fading, his thoughts blurring to nothing as primal instincts seized control.

He feared what would happen if he risked waiting, and was terrified of what he might do if he surrendered to his urges.

There was no way for him to win, and no way for her to get out of this unscathed.

"I'm sorry," he croaked, defeated. "I should have known they'd pull some shit like this."

Bronwyn shook her head, causing the soft spikes of her pixie cut to brush her neck. "Don't be sorry."

She slowly walked towards him, completely unravelling his resolve and tearing down his strength as she undid the belt of her robe and let it fall open, baring her curves to him.

He stared at her, his brow furrowing. "You don't want to do this."

She smiled softly.

"I do want to do this."

Her eyes warmed as she gazed at him.

"I've always wanted you, Maverick."

CHAPTER 16

Bronwyn was nervous as heck, but she refused to let it show as she stood before Maverick, bared to him, every inch of her aware of his eyes on her. Her skin felt too hot and tight as she waited for him to say something or do something, whether it was to push her away or take her into his arms. She had wanted this for so long, and she knew it wasn't the way he wanted things to be between them, but she wasn't afraid of him. She trusted him.

He needed her.

The evidence of that was clear as day in his shorts.

Heat scalded her cheeks as she glanced at the outline of his erection, seeped into her blood as she raked her gaze up the ropes of his stomach, slowing to savour the sight of him. Her eyes snagged on every bruise and cut that marred his honed muscles and worry flooded her veins, but it wasn't strong enough to win against the fire that seared her as she recalled how majestic he had been in the cage. The thought of watching him fighting had sickened her at first, but the moment he had sprung into action, fear had fallen away and she had been mesmerised. Every blow he had landed had stoked a powerful and primal response in her, had aroused her and flooded her with a fierce, aching need that only he could sate.

So when she said she wanted him, she *really* wanted him. She had never been more on fire for him.

This wasn't quite the way she had imagined their first time would go, but they had no choice. They could have a do-over once they were free, could start again if he needed that.

Maverick's grey eyes raked over her, his pupils dilating to darken them with hunger that excited her, had her pulse pounding faster and her body coming alive, eager for his touch.

On a low, thrilling growl, he swept her into his arms and turned with her, pinned her against the wall and kissed her hard, immediately proving how different he was to the male he had once been. He had never kissed the females he had been with after the fights.

She melted into it, relaxing so he didn't sense her nerves. She didn't want him to mistake them for fear of him. She wasn't nervous about doing this.

She was nervous about the fact they were being watched.

She pushed that to the back of her mind as she gripped Maverick's shoulders and kissed him.

It wasn't hard to forget everything but him existed when he palmed her bare bottom and lifted her, slid between her thighs and made her wrap her legs around his waist. He groaned as he pressed against her, every delicious, hard inch of his body meeting hers delighting her too.

When he shifted his hands closer together, she gasped and shivered. His fingers brushed her plush petals again, sending another thrill chasing through her, and when he growled, that thrill turned to fire that burned up her blood, turning her inhibitions to ashes.

She closed her eyes and sank against the wall as he stroked her, teasing her, another feral growl pealing from his lips. She knew the reason for that hungry snarl. She was slick for him, had been aching for him from the moment she had been pushed into the room and had found herself standing in the middle of her dream of him.

Only this time it was real.

He removed one hand from her and tightened his grip with the other, holding her in place, and her heart drummed as he shoved at his shorts, anticipation swirling like a maelstrom inside her as she realised what he was doing. She dropped her gaze between them, bit back a groan as she saw a flash of his hard cock as he fisted it, and then he pressed forwards, stealing himself from view.

She cried out as he pinned her to the wall and guided himself into her, as the blunt head breached her and he drove forwards, claiming her in one forceful thrust.

He grunted as he gripped her backside and pounded into her, buried his head in her neck and slammed her into the wall with each powerful plunge of his cock. Electric shivers raced through her, stealing the pain away as need built inside her, as it hit her that it was Maverick inside her. Maverick claiming her.

She moaned and clawed at his neck, couldn't help herself as his strokes lengthened and he began to slow them, growing gentler with her. She locked her senses on him, felt him calming as he moved inside her, and she knew the reason why.

He was her fated mate.

He had been consumed by fear that he would hurt her, but he couldn't. Every instinct he possessed was probably screaming at him to be gentle with her. Tender. She opened her eyes and looked at him as he pulled back, as he gazed at her, a softness to his grey eyes that warmed her.

Made her feel loved.

She loved him too, and while she was enjoying this slower moment, she couldn't let it last. They had to make this look convincing. The people watching them didn't want to see him being gentle with her. It wouldn't satisfy them. They were doing this to break him after all, to humiliate him and ruin things between them.

"Harder," she whispered, giving him a look she hoped he could read, one that reminded him why they were here, doing this.

Their freedom depended upon it.

He frowned, that soft look in his eyes going nowhere, and for a heartbeat, she was sure he wouldn't do it, but then he twisted with her and set her backside down on the table. He hesitated as he gripped the shoulder of her robe, gave her an apologetic look, and yanked it down, exposing her. The flat of his hand against her chest was like a brand and she bit back a groan as he shoved her down onto the table, and pulled her robe down to her elbows, baring all of her.

She arched into his touch as he palmed her breasts and thrust into her, taking her harder again. Gods. She could feel every inch of him as he filled her, as he claimed her body, possessing her completely. She couldn't hold back the moan that tumbled from her lips as he dragged her to the edge of the table and held her there, tightly gripping her hip as he took her.

Maverick growled and she looked at him, saw in his eyes it was mostly for show, but it still thrilled her. She clenched around him, ripping a grunt from him, and he bared fangs and hooked his arms under her knees, opening her to him. He gazed down at the point where they joined as he forced her legs further apart, as he drove deeper into her, each forceful thrust shaking the table and making her breasts bounce. Sweat slicked his torso, caressing muscles that flexed as he gripped her harder.

His handsome face darkened, another grunt leaving his lips as he quickened his pace. Pleasure built inside her with each slide and retreat, had her losing control as she reached for release, so close she could almost touch it. She strained for it, breathing harder, faster, desperate to find it.

It hit her in a blinding flash and she cried out as she arched off the table, as her entire body quivered and heat rolled through her, leaving her breathless.

Maverick snarled and pulled out of her, flipped her onto her front on her knees so her breasts and cheek pressed against the cold metal. He mounted the table behind her, twisted the sleeves of her robe around his hand, binding her arms together behind her back, and speared her again, a grunt leaving him as he filled her. Her breath blasted back at her from the table as he held her immobile, pushing her towards another release with each punishing thrust of his thick cock.

His other hand came down on her backside, his fingers pressing into her buttock, gripping it tightly as he raised one leg and planted his foot against the table on the other side of her shin. She groaned as he pounded into her, taking her harder again, rocking her forwards with every powerful plunge of his shaft. Maverick snarled in response and quickened his pace again, his balls slapping her with each frantic meeting of their bodies.

Her cries mingled with his grunts as she passed through the haze of her release and soared towards another, the feel of him dominating her triggering her own primal instincts, making her hungry for more. She growled and he snarled in response, answering her demand for more with longer strokes that drove her out of her mind.

He released her backside and yanked back on her arms, lifting her top half off the table as his free hand delved between her thighs.

Bronwyn shouted her release as it hit her, couldn't hold back her cries of pleasure as it detonated inside her, rocking her harder this time. Her thighs quivered as Maverick pressed deep inside her and roared. His cock pulsed and he thrust hard and deep, sharp plunges to the hilt as he filled her with his hot seed, grunting each time. She groaned with each jet, each fierce throb of his length, and sagged against the table as he released her arms to hold her hips. He groaned in time with her as he held her on him, as he remained buried inside her long after he was done.

When he finally pulled out of her, she sank onto her belly on a breathless sigh.

Maverick caught her arm and pulled her around to face him, up into a sitting position at the end of the table. He seized her nape and kissed her. Hard. But it was soft, spoke to her and told her everything he couldn't while people were listening in. He was sorry. She wasn't.

"You didn't hurt me," she whispered against his lips, low enough that his sensitive hearing would pick it up but hopefully the microphones wouldn't.

He stiffened.

She skimmed her hands over his damp pectorals as she sensed the shift in his emotions.

He opened his mouth, closed it and kissed her again, harder this time.

When he broke the kiss, he whispered, "Play along. I'll get you out of this. I swear. When you're free, call Rune. Warn my pride."

The warmth filling her turned to ice as she realised something.

He meant to gain her freedom for her and he intended to do it by sacrificing himself.

She wasn't going to allow that.

They were leaving together.

She wanted that forever he had promised her.

CHAPTER 17

Bronwyn tensed when the door buzzed and opened, and even though he knew it was all done for show when she shoved him off her and hastily covered herself, it still cut Maverick like a blade.

She cast her golden eyes down at her legs as she sat on the edge of the table, wrapped her arms around her stomach and refused to look at him.

Gods, he was a monster.

Not only because he had taken her hard and for the hunters to see, but because he had taken something else from her. Her first time should have been gentler, definitely should have been private rather than broadcast for the disgusting humans to watch.

"Move it," the dark-haired male at the door grunted and waved a gun at both of them.

Maverick fixed his shorts and glared at the human, bared his fangs and made sure the man knew he was pushing his luck. The only thing stopping Maverick from launching at him to take him down was the fact Bronwyn would be caught in the crossfire. He had to be patient and wait for the right moment to strike.

Preferably one where Winnie wouldn't be exposed to danger.

A male could dream.

He slid a look at her and she glanced at him, a flush of colour on her cheeks that wasn't anger. Her honey-coloured eyes heated as she held his gaze, spoke to him on a primal level, one where he wasn't quite master.

There was hunger in that look. Need. He could feel it in her too and it drove him crazy all over again, and gave him hope.

She still wanted him.

That had to be a good sign, right?

A sign that he hadn't just messed everything up?

He had tried his hardest to be gentle with her and make it look convincing, had tempered his need and somehow controlled his darker urges. Although, he wasn't sure somehow was the right word. Something about her had tamed that part of him. The moment he had gotten inside her, a calm had come over him, the part of him he had feared would rise to the fore falling away instead, replaced by a powerful need to please her, to savour the connection and even deepen it.

Maverick's gaze shifted to her neck and he shivered as he thought about when he had been on the table with her, how he hadn't been able to take his eyes off that spot on her nape or his mind off the urge to sink his fangs into it and bind them as mates.

"I said move it." The human made the mistake of lunging for Bronwyn.

On a vicious black growl, Maverick caught the male's arm and twisted it hard enough to snap bone. The human bellowed in agony, sending satisfaction rolling through Maverick and tugging a grin from him.

"Son of a bitch." Another male launched into the room.

Drove the butt of his gun into Maverick's temple hard enough to have the room pitching and wobbling and fading towards black. He fell into Bronwyn and she gasped, grabbed hold of him and stopped him from hitting the deck. Maverick bit out a ripe curse as he tried to shake off the blow.

Stupid move.

So much for biding his time.

Apparently, he couldn't control his aggression when Winnie was in danger. He focused on dialling back his need to protect her, clawing back control and breathing through the urge to utterly destroy the two human males now in the room with her. All in good time.

If he got into a fight in here, they would close the doors again, trapping them. He needed to wait until they were in transit to the cells before he made his move, and even then it was risky. The collar could easily take him down in his current state. He was tired from the fight and from being with Winnie, and now he was a little groggy from being struck by the gun. It wouldn't take much for the hunters to incapacitate him and then Winnie would be left defenceless.

Maverick rolled his neck as best he could as he pushed back onto his feet, itching to get the damned collar off now that he was hyper-aware of it again. He eyed the hunters, wondering if either of them had one of the devices that controlled it. Doubtful. They didn't look like senior staff.

The one Maverick had injured muttered about his arm as he left the room, a new dark-haired hunter filing in to take his place. This one smiled at Winnie. Maverick recognised him from the video she had saved on her laptop. It was the hunter who had cut her brother and pretended to be hurting him, forcing her hand.

She growled at him, her agitation flowing around Maverick as she dropped to her feet and came to face him.

"Good to see you again too." The hunter grinned at her and pulled out a blade, flipping it around in his hand as he kept his eyes locked on hers. "Did you like that little act of mine?"

Bronwyn spat in his face. "You bastard!"

The male wiped it away.

Maverick caught her arm before she could do something foolish like attacking him. She glared over her shoulder at him and yanked her arm free of his grip, breathing hard as rage and hurt shone in her eyes.

"Move it, or I'll pump your boyfriend with fifty thousand volts." The hunter waved the knife in her face.

Bronwyn tensed and threw a nervous look at Maverick. He nodded, silently telling her it was fine for her to do as the hunter wanted. Eager to get going now that he knew this male had what he needed—a controller for his collar.

Maverick eyed him as he led the way, studying everything about him. Killing him wouldn't be a chore. Winnie needed some form of closure, revenge against the hunters who had tricked her, and he would give that to her in a heartbeat, and gain his freedom at the same time.

He filed out of the holding room behind Bronwyn, aware of the hunter behind him. Mostly because the male was enjoying prodding him in the back with the muzzle of his assault rifle.

Several other hunters were waiting in the wide plain white corridor, fell into step with him and Winnie as they moved through the compound, following the maze of hallways. Maverick tried to get the lay of the land, scouting out every route that branched off the main avenue through the building. He could sense more humans in the distance down those hallways. Escaping was going to be difficult.

A young hunter eyed Bronwyn and then the male who walked on the other side of her. "Did you see the way she took that pounding?"

Maverick scowled at him and then the other hunter when he answered.

"Did I? I almost nutted just watching her get boned. How twisted is it that I'm attracted to a shifter of all things?"

Maverick growled when Bronwyn tensed and he sensed her shame, saw it in how she lowered her head and curled inwards, holding herself. He hated that she had been forced to do that with him, that she had seen that side of him and had been subjected to it.

And that these fiends had watched.

Had seen her in the wildest throes of passion.

Something only he should have seen.

The dark-haired hunter flicked a look over his shoulder at Maverick and then the two younger hunters. "Dial it back. All of you."

The youngest hunter shrugged. "I'm just saying. I'd like to get up on that table and do her like that. Think they'd let me?"

The male held his hands in front of his hips and gyrated.

Maverick slammed a fist into the side of his head, knocking him into the wall. His head cracked off it and he went down hard, out for the count.

Lightning shot down Maverick's spine and he bellowed as electricity arced along his bones, dropped to his knees and grabbed the collar as his body bowed forwards.

"Maverick." Bronwyn turned and reached for him, growled when a hunter grabbed her and stopped her. Her face twisted and she battered him with her elbow. "Let go of me. Stop hurting him!"

The radio on the dark-haired hunter's belt crackled and then a voice came over it. "Readying the helicopters for departure. Wheels up in one hour. Briefing in thirty in the hangar. Expected return time with the assets is just after dawn."

Maverick gritted his teeth against the electricity surging through him, anger blazing hot on its heels as he realised the person on the radio was talking about heading to Black Ridge while it was dark. Saint wouldn't be prepared for the onslaught. They would catch his pride and the cougars while they were sleeping.

He couldn't let that happen.

He drew on every last shred of his strength and snarled as he lumbered onto his feet, fighting the effects of the collar. The dark-haired hunter narrowed his eyes on him and shifted his thumb over another button on the small device he gripped.

The one that would shoot Maverick with a hefty dose of tranquiliser.

Bronwyn noticed it too and threw a hard elbow into the face of the hunter who was restraining her, breaking his nose, and launched at the dark-haired male. She slammed into him, knocking the device flying, and shoving him off-balance. The hunter tipped backwards with her, found his footing at the last second and grappled with her as she growled and lashed out at him.

The hunter seized her by her throat and threw her away from him.

Maverick exploded into action, not wasting a second. He took down the hunter who had held her and dodged right as one of the pair behind him opened fire. One of the bullets ripped through his shoulder and he grunted as heat bloomed over his left deltoid, the hot slide of blood down his bare skin dragging the darker part of him to the fore. He made fast work of the next hunter, snapped his neck with a vicious twist of his hands, and set his sights on the dark-haired one.

The male grabbed Bronwyn again and Maverick bared fangs at him as she wrestled against his hold. The sight of his fated female being manhandled by another male, the scent of her fear as it mingled with her peaches and cream fragrance, hurled Maverick off the deep end.

He roared as he rushed the hunter, not giving him a chance to use the blade he brought up towards her throat, catching him before he could get it close to her. He smashed his palm against the hunter's fist, knocking the knife away from Bronwyn, and barrelled into him as she twisted away from the male, leaving him open.

Maverick slammed him into the floor, landing on top of him, and grabbed his head. He lifted it and drove it into the concrete with enough force that bone cracked. The hunter went limp and Maverick turned on another vicious snarl as he heard the remaining two hunters fighting Bronwyn.

She fought valiantly, hitting them with untrained punches that were powerful enough to deal damage to the male who was trying to pin her and get hold of her. The second male readied his gun again, aiming it at her, wavering as his companion kept getting in the way of his shot.

Maverick sprang at him, cocking his fist at the same time, and drove it into his face as he landed, knocking the male out.

The hunter's finger hit the trigger on his way down and Maverick grunted as a bullet ripped through his side, just above his right hip. He plastered his hand against it and staggered into the wall to his right, breathed hard as he fought the pain that swept through him like a white-hot inferno.

"Maverick!" Bronwyn twisted and slammed the hunter she was wrestling into the wall. His head cracked off it and he slid to the floor when she released him, out cold. She hurried to Maverick, concern warming her golden eyes as her brow furrowed and she looked him over. "Is it bad?"

He swallowed hard and shook his head. "I'll live."

But he was weakening. The fight had left him tired and sore enough, had depleted him, and taking two nasty hits wasn't helping matters. He could feel his strength bleeding from him. They had to move quickly if they were going to stop the hunters.

"The hangar. We need to find the hangar." Maverick clutched his side, his fingers slipping in the blood.

Bronwyn looked around her, eyes darting over everything, and when she hurried off behind him, he eased his back against the wall to keep an eye on her.

"What are you doing?" He frowned at her as she grabbed the knife from the concrete floor and bent over.

She nicked the edge of her robe around six inches up from the hem and ripped it all the way around, tearing a strip off, and then tossed the knife away. "We need to stop the bleeding."

He sagged into the wall as she hurried back to him. "We don't have time for this."

"We do." Her eyes flashed fire at him and he felt like a bastard when he saw the worry in them—the fear. He sighed and surrendered, couldn't deny his female anything that would make her feel better and would give her hope. She tore a piece off one end of the strip of material and folded it. "Hold this in place."

She brought it to his hand.

Maverick swallowed and eased his hand away from his side, hated the way fear flitted across her eyes and she gasped as she saw the wound. "I'll be fine, Winnie. It went straight through. Is probably already healing."

She gave him a look that revealed how deeply she doubted that, how her thoughts were treading dark paths that were upsetting her.

He placed his hand over hers when she pressed the wad of material to his side and she glanced at him again, lingering this time.

He lifted his other hand and brushed his knuckles across her cheek as he whispered, "I swear. I'll be fine. We'll get through this."

"Together." There was a demand in that one word, an order he felt down to his soul. She knew him better than he had thought, had clearly seen straight through him back in the holding room. Now her desperate desire to fight beside him, to protect him made sense. She didn't want him to sacrifice himself for her. She wanted them both to survive this and that look in her eyes told him that she wanted forever with him.

And gods, he felt blessed.

Undeserving of that love that shone in her eyes.

But at the same time he craved it, savoured it and wanted more.

He wanted forever with her.

He wanted to look into her eyes and keep seeing all that love directed at him.

Because it made him believe he could be a better male, could be what she deserved.

He nodded. "Together."

She wrapped the rest of the material around his waist, making only a single tight pass with it before she tied it above his other hip. It would be enough to stop the blood loss.

"What about your shoulder?" She looked at it.

He shook his head. "Just a graze. It'll be fine."

She hurried off again and he watched her as he pressed his fingers to his side and grimaced at how sore it was. At least it was slowly going numb, shouldn't be too much of a distraction in the fight ahead.

When she returned to him this time, she had the controller and the radio.

Bronwyn peered at the buttons on the small black device. "How do I—"

"I've got this." Maverick was quick to take it from her when her finger hovered dangerously close to the button that would inject him with a tranquiliser. He pressed the button for the release on his collar and sighed as it snapped open.

Before he could grab it and hurl it away from him, Bronwyn seized hold of it and threw it along the hallway.

His gaze snagged on something there. A camera mounted on the ceiling pointed towards a corridor that intersected the one they were in. He looked around them, seeking another one, fearing that someone would have witnessed the fight, and spied one at the other end of the corridor. So much for getting to the hangar without a fight. The moment they set foot near the corner of the hallway, they were going to be spotted.

Or were they?

He looked at Winnie.

"I have an idea."

CHAPTER 18

"I'm not convinced this is a good idea."

That was around the tenth time Bronwyn had said that since he had made her strip one of the hunters and put their clothes on, and take the gun, knife, radio and controller. She had given him a look when he had retrieved the collar and put it back on.

One that had asked whether he had lost his mind.

"Look. To these cameras, you just look like a hunter escorting me to the cellblock. I don't hear any alarms, so it's working, right?" He flicked a glance back at her.

Cursed in his head.

She did look damn fine in that outfit.

Tight black combat clothing suited her, and the gun was a nice addition, made her look a little badass as she waved it at him.

"Eyes forward." The corners of her lips quirked in a way that said part of her was enjoying this charade too, or maybe she was just enjoying the view.

He growled and wished he could tell her something similar as she raked her gaze over him, igniting his blood. The feel of her eyes on his bare flesh was enough to have him wanting to find a quiet corner where there were no cameras so he could kiss her. Softly this time. Reverently. So she knew how much he loved her and needed her, and that he could be gentle for her.

If she would give him a chance.

He needed her to give him a chance.

Things between them hadn't started well, but they could be better. He could make them better.

Fate didn't seem to want to give him a chance to prove that.

He turned the corner in the corridor and came face to face with Andrew.

The bear's golden eyes shifted from him to Winnie and widened. "What the—"

He reached for his pocket just as Bronwyn noticed him, her gasp reaching Maverick's ears. The male didn't get the chance to press the button on the controller he pulled from his trousers. She beat him to it, striking the button on the one she clutched, popping his collar open before her brother could hit him with fifty thousand volts.

The collar clattered to the floor at Maverick's bare feet and he launched at Andrew on a vicious growl, unable to hold himself back as Bronwyn's hurt hit him all over again, the shift in her mood triggering a violent response in him.

A need to protect her.

Andrew pulled something else from the waistband of his trousers and aimed it at him.

Maverick's entire body lit up in agony as the small darts pierced his flesh and the wires attached to the device delivered a punishing blast of electricity. He went down hard, juddering as lightning pulsed through him, sound warbling in his ears as he struggled to withstand it.

"No!" Bronwyn yelled and he tried to fix his senses on her, but the taser made it impossible as it hit him with another cycle of electricity, pushing him towards darkness.

She appeared before him, shaking in his vision as he shuddered, and struck her brother hard enough to make him lose his grip on the device. She fumbled for it, a desperate look on her face, and shrieked when Andrew grabbed her hair from behind and hauled her backwards. Her fingers briefly brushed the taser before she was pulled away from it and her hands flew to his wrist as her face twisted in agony.

Maverick thought he growled.

Wasn't sure.

Everything felt as if it was getting tangled and twisted as lightning continued to pump into him, smell and sound blurring together, sight knotting with taste, and he wasn't sure when the floor had started pitching and rolling.

Bronwyn's desperate growl spurred him to keep fighting the effects, had him focusing all of his will on inching one hand towards a wire that was close to it. His eyes watered as his fingers shook violently, the way his muscles clamped down on his bones with each fifty-thousand-volt blast making it hard to move. He pushed himself to keep trying, even as the darkness encroaching at the corners of his vision began to spread more rapidly.

His female needed him.

She valiantly fought her brother, managing to break free again, and lunged for the taser. Knocked it flying as she hit the concrete floor hard thanks to her brother kicking her in the back. It skidded towards Maverick and landed near his knees.

Bronwyn scrambled for the wires instead.

She grabbed them just as her brother seized hold of her again and yanked them with her as he hauled her back to him, tugging them free of Maverick's chest.

Andrew growled at her as he realised what she had done.

Maverick roared at him as he backhanded her.

She hit the wall hard and slumped to the floor, and fear hit him like a truck, had his heart pounding in his ears as he stared at her, all of his senses locked on her. Relief hit him just as hard as he saw her chest move, a soft inhale that told him she had only blacked out.

But it did nothing to calm his mood or leash his temper.

He exploded from the floor, slamming into Andrew as the male looked ready to level another kick at his own sister and ripping him away from her. Andrew grunted as Maverick twisted with him and drove his back into the wall, pinning him there.

"You're a son of a bitch, you know that?" he growled in Andrew's face, anger getting the better of him, his blood on fire as he thought about everything Andrew had put her through. "I ought to put you in the ground."

"But you won't." Andrew smiled coldly and Maverick bared fangs at him but couldn't deny the male was right.

Killing Andrew would hurt her and Maverick had done that enough already. He didn't want to hurt her again, didn't want to make this whole experience worse for her, but the colder, harder part of him also knew he couldn't let Andrew go.

The bear knew where his pride lived, had been handing shifters over to Archangel hunters for years now, building this sick empire for himself. He couldn't let Andrew get away with that.

"You know. Back then… I hated you." Andrew spat each word, his expression darkening. "I hated you for taking my sister from me."

"I never took Winnie from you." Maverick scowled at the male. "Winnie loves you. Nothing can change that. You've put her through hell… hurt her… but deep inside she still loves you."

Andrew snorted. "She loves *you*. I saw the way she looked at you even back then. She loves you… because you're strong."

Maverick shook his head. "She's my fated female. She wouldn't have known it back then… Hell, I didn't acknowledge it back then… but she is my true mate. I love her. Christ, I would have loved her even if she hadn't been made for me. Your sister is a kind, beautiful soul. A light in this dark world… and it pisses me off that you can't see that."

The bear's face blackened, his eyes slowly narrowing on Maverick's as a growl rumbled from him.

"And what kind of fickle female do you think Winnie is to believe she doesn't have room in her heart for more than one person? She proved how much she loved you by going with you rather than with me and Rune." Maverick shoved his hand against the male's chest and stepped back from him, unable to believe the things Andrew was saying and on the verge of striking him for painting Winnie in such a bad light. "She proved it by bringing me here because she believed you were in danger and this was the only way to save you."

He shook his head again, unsure what to do with Andrew as he struggled to rein in his dark urge to surrender to his need to lash out at him, and unsure whether he could make the male see just how special, and loving, his sister was. He had the feeling he was wasting his breath.

Really had that feeling when fire bloomed just above the gunshot wound on his hip and he looked down.

Stared at Andrew's fist where it pressed into his side.

Grunted when the bastard pulled it back and tugged the small knife free of his flesh with a wet sucking sound.

Red veiled the world and Maverick roared as he cocked his fist and struck Andrew hard across the jaw, snapping his head to his right, and then hit him again as he was going down. Andrew swung blindly for him, his elbow struck the wall and his arm lurched off course, heading back at himself instead.

Maverick flinched as the blade Andrew gripped cut a slash across the base of his neck.

Bit out a curse as blood gushed from the wound.

He dropped to his knees beside the male and pressed his hand to the wound as Andrew's wide golden eyes landed on him, wild with pain and fear. Maverick pressed hard against the small gash, his hand slipping around in the blood.

Swore again, aiming it at Andrew this time.

The bear's actions grew sluggish as he fumbled for his throat, his eyes going glazed.

"Dammit. Don't you dare die on me." Because he didn't want to have to tell Bronwyn her brother was dead. She would assume he had done it, would see him as the monster he was, a male so callous and unfeeling that he would kill someone she loved.

He pressed harder against the wound as Andrew slumped against the floor and stared at the male's face and then the blood pooling beneath him. His hope leached from him at the same rate as that blood poured from Andrew.

Maverick hung his head forwards, let his hands fall from Andrew's neck and growled out another curse.

He wiped his hands on Andrew's shirt and frowned as he glanced at the male's trouser pocket and spotted something silver. He took the locket and stared at it, sighed and curled his fingers around it as he stood, trying to think of what he was going to tell Bronwyn when she came around.

He turned and froze as he found her staring at her brother, pale as a ghost, her eyes enormous.

His fingers tightened around the locket as his heart clenched and the tears that trembled on her dark eyelashes made his chest constrict. "How much did you see?"

"Enough," she whispered, a lost look in her eyes.

"How much did you hear?" His heart drummed a sickening rhythm against his chest as he recalled what he had told her brother.

He loved her.

Her eyes shifted to lock with his. "Enough."

Maverick swallowed hard and went to her, held the locket out to her and waited for her to take it. She slipped her hand into his and pulled herself up onto her feet instead, and then glanced down at their joined hands.

"I'm sorry," he murmured.

"It wasn't your fault." She smiled briefly, there and gone in a heartbeat, and he could feel the pain in her, knew it was going to take her some time to get over losing her brother and the things Andrew had done and said to her, but if she let him, Maverick would be with her every second of it.

Her hand slipped from his and she gazed at the locket in her palm as she sighed.

She curled her fingers around it and slipped it into her pocket.

Looked at him.

"Let's go home."

Home.

That single word gave him hope, buoyed him up and chased his fears away, making him feel as if that future he needed with Winnie was still on the cards.

He took hold of her hand and started walking with her again, drawing her away from her brother and standing on that side of her so she didn't have to see him. He breathed a little easier when they rounded a corner, but tensed again when he spotted a glass panel in one of the walls ahead of him. He approached it slowly, cautiously, his senses checking ahead of him.

It was empty.

The tension flowed from him again and he glanced into the security room as they passed the window, staring at the monitors that revealed the hangar and the soldiers gathered in it, preparing to depart on helicopters that would take them to Black Ridge.

Home.

She had called it that. She had made it sound as if it was her home too now, that she would stay with him and become a part of his life—a part that felt vital to him.

He wanted to go home with her and start that new life with her.

But first, they needed to keep that home safe.

And make it out of this place alive.

CHAPTER 19

Bronwyn clutched the assault rifle as she hurried along a stark white corridor behind Maverick. He bent his dark head towards the plastic sign he had ripped from a wall, one that had a map of the building on it, and then stilled and lifted his head. When he canted it, she listened too, straining to hear what he had.

"This way." He tossed the sign away, grabbed her wrist and pulled her with him, forcing her into a run.

Her gaze darted to the strip of black material wrapped around his waist and then lifted to the spot above it, and her stomach turned as she stared at the crimson trail that tracked down his hip from the knife wound there. She peered at the strong hand that gripped her arm and wrenched her eyes away. Blood stained it. Her brother's blood.

Sickness brewed, acid forming to scour her insides raw as she replayed that moment all over again and felt as if she was reliving it. She had come around to a buzzing head and Maverick arguing with Andrew, had wanted to say something but the pain had been too much.

And then Andrew had stabbed him.

She had seen the moment Maverick had snapped.

His grey eyes had rapidly darkened like a thunderstorm and he had reacted in an instant, striking her brother twice.

She kept wondering what might have happened if Andrew hadn't tried to hit him again with the knife. If things had gone even slightly differently, would her brother still be alive? She hadn't wanted him to die, hurt right down to her soul as she thought about the fact he was gone. Some part of her had clung to the belief she could redeem him somehow, had dared to hope that he would come around and correct the terrible things he had done if she just kept trying to reach him.

Had believed that she could make him see how deeply she loved him.

Maverick had tried to make him see it, but the look on her brother's face had crushed her hope. Andrew had severed all ties with her, had killed whatever feelings he'd had for her, and had made up his mind about her feelings towards him. He had convinced himself that she didn't love him and nothing she could have said or done would have changed that.

It wasn't a comfort.

She tensed as Maverick pulled her behind a wall at a junction in the corridor and flattened his back against it. He leaned away from her and peered around the corner.

When he eased back and looked her way, he stilled and lingered, his grey eyes holding hers. The cold in them turned to warmth laced with fear and a hint of despair as he edged closer to her and turned, lifted his hand and swept his fingers across her cheek, spreading moisture across it.

She quickly lifted her hand and wiped the tears she hadn't noticed away.

"I'm sorry," he husked.

Bronwyn shook her head. He kept saying that, but there was really no need for him to apologise. She had seen everything. She had witnessed how hard he had tried to convince her brother and how he hadn't been able to bring himself to hurt Andrew. Maverick had wanted to try to save him and it had been for her sake. He hadn't wanted her to hurt any worse than she already had been and she appreciated that.

Because it revealed how deeply he loved her.

He had every reason to hate her brother, to want him dead, but he had given him a chance to redeem himself, had tried to deal with him without resorting to violence.

She slung the strap of the gun over her shoulder and placed her hand over Maverick's on her arm, held his gaze and hoped he saw in it that she didn't blame him for what had happened. She didn't hold him responsible in any way. Her brother had made his choice, and in the end, he had paid for it.

Bronwyn eased closer to him, tiptoed and surrendered to the urge that ran through her, pressing her lips to his as her eyes slipped shut. His kiss was soft, hesitant, and then he slid his arm around her waist and tugged her closer, angled his head and kissed her deeper, stirring warmth in her with each brush of his lips across hers. She savoured the kiss and that warmth, how it curled through her to ease her fears and reassured her.

Mourned the loss of both when Maverick eased back.

He gazed down at her, his grey eyes warm and soft.

His throat worked on a hard swallow.

Maverick opened his mouth, snapped it closed and looked away from her again. "We're here."

Her heart drummed faster, the fear rolling up on her again. A burst of adrenaline shot through her as she stretched her senses around her and detected more than two dozen humans nearby.

Maverick glanced at her again. "Ready?"

"No." She gripped his hand, all of her feelings lodging in her throat to make it impossible for her to say what she needed to tell him before they both lost their minds and tried to take on dozens of soldiers with only one gun.

An alarm rang, the high shrieking wail of it piercing her sensitive ears and making her flinch.

"Stick close." Maverick tugged her to him, planted a brief, hard kiss on her lips and then he was moving.

Bronwyn shouldered her assault rifle, not really sure what she was doing with it, but willing to give it a go. It couldn't be that hard to use. She had watched plenty of action movies in her years. Enough that she eyed it as they hurried along a corridor, towards the swarm of humans she had sensed.

The safety was off.

That was a good start.

The smell of oil and fuel hit her, together with the scent of human sweat and gunpowder, and she breathed through a momentary spike in panic as she followed Maverick out into a dark corner of an enormous hangar.

The entire wall off to her right was open to the night, two large black helicopters parked there beneath the moonlight, their rotor blades lazily turning.

Maverick pulled her down behind a stack of black cases and wooden crates, and leaned towards the edge of their makeshift cover. He ducked back again and she tensed as she sensed why. A male dressed in black fatigues similar to the ones she wore strolled around the corner, didn't notice them as he adjusted his grip on his gun and sighed.

Maverick launched from the shadows, clamped a hand over his mouth and dragged him down into cover.

She flinched as he snapped the hunter's neck and pushed him away in one fluid move, snagging his gun in the process. He checked it over, looking far more comfortable with the weapon than she was with hers, and then glanced at her. She dragged her eyes away from the dead hunter.

Concern flickered in Maverick's gaze.

She managed a smile, hoping to alleviate his worry. "I'll be fine."

"You don't have to kill anyone, Winnie," he whispered. "Leave it all to me."

She appreciated that, but she also hated how weak it made her feel. These were hunters, humans intent on hurting people she cared about, enslaving them and putting them through hell, all for the sake of entertainment. She shouldn't be hesitating to kill them, but she was. The thought of shooting them had her feeling sick all over again.

But she couldn't let Maverick fight alone.

She couldn't let him shoulder this burden too.

Not when she had vowed that they would make it through this together.

She readied her gun and drew down a steadying breath, steeled her heart and nodded, silently telling Maverick that she was as prepared as she was going to get.

Bronwyn focused on the dozens of soldiers behind her.

Although she really wasn't sure Maverick had thought this through.

That feeling grew as Maverick rushed from behind the stack of crates, keeping low, the gun clutched close to his chest as he raced for the next block of cover. When he reached it, he looked back at her and frowned, a confused edge to his gaze. Like hell she was running across open ground, even when she was dressed like one of the soldiers. She was staying firmly behind cover at all times.

Maverick frowned and then twisted towards the cases and boxes. He poked his head up, gaze scanning everything in a fast sweep before he ducked back down behind cover. He motioned to her, signalling something off to her left, his look one of pure worry.

Bronwyn eased onto her toes in a crouch and came to face the crates and peered to her right, towards whatever Maverick had spotted.

Three soldiers.

They were doing a lap of the hangar, heading in her direction. A patrol like the one Maverick had killed.

The alarm continued to blare, dampening her hearing and making it impossible for her to tell what they were saying as they talked. She looked back at Maverick, unsure what to do—break cover and rush to him, or wait for them to reach her and attack.

Her eyes widened.

She waved her hand towards the two males who were heading straight for him, would be right on top of him in only a few seconds.

Maverick turned and loosed a spray of bullets, nailing both of them.

The whole hangar erupted into action.

The trio that had been heading for her opened fire on Maverick and he ducked behind cover, waited for them to stop firing before he popped back up again and unleashed another hail of bullets. Fear blasted through her, shaking her, but the sight of Maverick standing there bare-chested and shooting an automatic rifle provided a powerful distraction, one that almost had her forgetting they were both in grave danger as she responded on a biological level where she wasn't quite master.

One of the men took cover and scooted towards her and Bronwyn panicked when she sensed him behind her, twisted and brought her rifle up, striking him hard in the side of his head with the butt of it. He went down on a muffled grunt.

Someone yelled, “There’s two of them.”

It ended on an agonised cry as Maverick nailed him in the shoulder and then that cry abruptly cut off as the next bullet ripped through his forehead. The male beside him lunged for him as he went down, caught himself as he clearly realised it was too late, and turned on Maverick, opening fire.

Maverick ducked behind cover and shrank lower in time with her as the other soldiers in the hangar opened fire too. He glanced at her, that look telling her to keep down. As if she was insane enough to do anything other than that. She wanted to survive this. She wanted them both to survive it.

He checked his gun and frowned, threw it away and waved his hand towards her. Rather than surrendering her own weapon, she stole the one from the man she had knocked out and tossed that across the open stretch of concrete to him. He inspected the clip and shoved it back into place, readied the weapon like a seasoned pro and drew down a deep breath.

She wanted to yell at him when he popped up from behind cover, firing off a few rounds.

He was going to get himself killed.

But then again, if they sat here and did nothing, that was a death sentence too.

Maverick waited for another break in gunfire before he raised his head and weapon enough to deal with the last hunter who was near her. She grimaced as the male fell into view, landing on his side with one arm stretched above his head and his sightless eyes fixed on her. She shuffled away from him a little and looked back at Maverick, watching him as he popped up and fired again, his shots more precise this time. He must have figured out the location of all the hunters in the hangar and was now picking them off.

Maybe they could survive this.

She tensed as the noise coming from the helicopters grew louder, their engines whining as the rotor blades began to beat the night air. Not good. She peeked over the top of the crates and her eyes widened as she saw close to ten hunters had broken away from the group and were running for the helicopters. Her eyes leaped to Maverick but he was too busy taking potshots at the hunters who had remained, was focused on them as they continued to fire back at him.

Not paying any attention to her.

Bronwyn stared at the helicopters.

She couldn't let them take off. Those soldiers would head to Black Ridge and everyone there would be in danger, and it would be all her fault.

She had to do something.

Her gaze fell to her gun.

She knew what she had to do.

Bronwyn lifted the weapon and aimed it as best she could, pointing it towards the helicopters. She depressed the trigger. Gasped as the gun immediately kicked upwards, the recoil far greater than she had anticipated. She sprayed bullets over the top of the helicopters, gritted her teeth and fought the weapon, bringing it down until the rounds were sort of hitting their target.

The soldiers that had been running for the helicopters ducked and kept low, slid behind cover as she overcompensated for the recoil and left a trail of holes in the side of one helicopter before the bullets pinged off the concrete, throwing dust up into the night air.

Some of those holes close to the rotor blades began to bleed smoke.

Several of the hunters pushed back onto their feet as she stopped firing, none of them making a break for the helicopters. They were running back towards her, yelling at each other.

The helicopter suddenly exploded in a blinding ball of fire, the shockwave catching the humans and hurling them towards her and Maverick, and heat rolled over her together with the scent of fuel.

Bronwyn stared wide-eyed at the hungry flames that devoured the two helicopters, the groans of the injured hunters distant to her ears as she tried to make herself believe what she had done.

It slowly dawned on her that they might have just won.

That fleeting feeling dissipated as more soldiers poured in from around the corner of the open end of the hangar and began firing in her and Maverick's direction, forcing them back behind cover.

She curled up as the bullets pinged off the cases and thudded into the crates, her heart racing in her throat as she cast a look at Maverick.

His brow furrowed as he stared across the twenty-foot strip of concrete that separated them, keeping low to the ground with his back against the crates. She could read that look in his eyes.

He wanted to come to her.

She shook her head.

It would be suicide.

Gasped as another wave of bullets tore into the cover behind her and forced Maverick back, further away from her.

She looked at him, locking gazes with him again, her heart aching now.

They weren't making it out of this alive.

CHAPTER 20

Maverick had to do something.

The need to reach Bronwyn seethed inside him, had his bear side and his human one restless as he gazed across the open stretch of concrete that separated them and looked as if it was miles to him. He wouldn't make it, not without taking a hit or two, and he was already injured. He would be no good to her if he was hurt worse than he was.

Or killed.

But the urge to protect her was strong, had him considering it as he looked at her, as he saw the hope in her eyes fading and felt the fear building in her.

She shrieked as more hunters turned their guns on the cover she was hiding behind, curled into a smaller ball and placed her hands over her head as she tucked it towards her knees. He growled and tensed, ached to launch across to her and hold her, needed to tell her everything was going to be all right.

Even when he feared it wouldn't be.

Maverick drew down a breath and held it, fought his instincts as her fated male and tried to be objective. The place where she was hiding was well defended, with metal shipping crates stacked in rows of two between her and the hunters. The bullets were only denting them, for now, which meant he had time to come up with a plan.

He poked his head over the top of his own stack of wooden crates and heavy-duty cases.

Ducked back down when he almost got his head blown off.

This wasn't good.

He had taken out a lot of the hunters, but the reinforcements that had arrived when Winnie had blown up the helicopters meant the number he was up against was more than double what it had been. This entire operation was far larger than he had imagined, but then he guessed the lure of hunting shifters and the promise of fat pay for delivering them to this arena was probably enticing to a lot of Archangel soldiers.

He bit out a curse.

Looked at Bronwyn again.

Sure that this was it, and he was never going to get to tell her that he loved her and wanted to be her mate, if she would have him.

She glanced at him too, uncurled a little as her honey-coloured eyes locked with his, her delicate features softening. Calm flowed through him as she said a thousand things to him without speaking a word, as he saw in her eyes that she loved him and she knew he loved her.

She pulled down a breath and he did too.

One last stand.

Maybe they could make it out of this.

He checked his rifle and cursed again when he saw there was only one bullet left. His gaze strayed back to Winnie. She frowned at the magazine he held and then looked at her gun, her brow furrowing. Before he could tell her not to, she had unclipped the magazine and it was sliding towards him across the concrete. He caught it and attached it to his rifle, drew down a breath.

This was it.

Maverick took one last look at Bronwyn and hoped that for once the universe was on his side. Fate owed him for all it had put him through.

He pushed to his feet and several soldiers immediately took aim at him. He picked one of them, swinging his rifle in their direction, and pulled the trigger. Nailed him between the eyes but the others opened fire before he could shift his aim to them, forcing him back behind cover. He waited for a break in fire and then popped up again, managing to take out another two, but it left a hell of a lot of hunters to go.

Maverick aimed at another one and growled when he depressed the trigger and nothing happened.

He sank back behind cover, tucking low as bullets tore into it behind him, and checked the magazine. Empty. He cast it aside and looked around, growled again when he couldn't see a single weapon within easy distance of him.

Behind him, the hunters hollered orders to close in and he could sense them flanking him and Winnie.

Fuck that bitch fate.

He looked at Winnie, aware this was the end.

But then cries and yells erupted behind him and the scent of human blood grew stronger, hitting him in a wave. What the hell? Maverick popped his head up again and frowned as several of the hunters turned away from him to face the direction of the burning helicopters. The staccato sound of gunfire rang in his ears together with his ragged breathing as he tried to make out what was happening.

The second he had an opening, he threw himself across the gap between him and Bronwyn and pulled her into his arms, shielding her with his body.

"What's happening?" she hollered above the noise of the battle raging behind them.

"Don't know."

Two roars sounded.

One bear.

One cougar.

Maverick twisted his upper body away from Bronwyn and looked over the lowest of the crates. Relief and disbelief blasted through him as he spotted the source of the commotion.

His pride.

And they weren't alone.

Rath and his brothers were with Saint, Lowe and Knox, and Rune. Lowe and Knox formed a formidable wall of black as they moved as one, using assault rifles they must have picked up from other soldiers in the base to take down any hunter who stood in their path. Rune was alternating between using his gun and his fists to fight his way deeper into the hangar. Saint had teamed up with Rath to cut a path in another direction. Rath's three cougar brothers were all heading in a line between them, using the crates and boxes as cover whenever needed.

They were spreading out.

Searching for him and Bronwyn.

Maverick grabbed her hand and pulled her with him as he broke right, towards the side of the hangar where they had entered it. He kept low, hoping she would do the same as bullets flew in all directions, forcing his pride and the cougars behind cover. Knox's handsome face twisted in dark lines as he expertly picked off several hunters with a handgun, providing cover for his twin as Lowe made a break for the next block of crates.

Rune appeared from behind a stack of cases, a shadow in the night dressed all in black, and Bronwyn tensed and gasped, her shock rolling into Maverick. She relaxed the moment she realised it was Rune.

Rune's pale blue eyes landed on him and then he growled as a hunter came out of nowhere, tackling him and knocking him face-first into the wall. Rune elbowed him in the side of his head and twisted, bringing his knee up into the male's side at the same time. He gripped the hunter by his hair and shoved his head down, smashing his knee into his face too, and tossed him away.

Casually swung the rifle he gripped towards the downed male and put a bullet in his head.

Rune grabbed another gun from the ground and slid into cover next to Maverick as hunters opened fire on him. He shoved the second gun at Maverick.

Maverick snatched it. "What the hell are you doing here?"

Rune glanced at him, the corners of his mouth twitching. "You didn't really think I would let you do this alone? You're my brother."

Not by blood, but hell, Rune was right. They were brothers and Maverick had never been so glad to see him.

Rune leaned forwards and peered around him. "You okay, Winnie?"

She emerged from behind Maverick, her free hand firmly gripping his biceps as she pressed closer to his bare back. "I'm fine. A little shaken, but I'm good. I thought we were dead there for a moment."

Rune cracked a rare grin at Maverick. "Good thinking blowing up that helicopter. One hell of a distress signal you sent up. We wouldn't have found you without it."

Maverick glanced over his shoulder at Bronwyn. "It wasn't me."

She smiled at Rune when the bear scowled at her.

"What the hell were you thinking?" he barked, the switch in his mood drawing a wider smile from her, one that was filled with affection.

It was typical of Rune to react differently to the fact Bronwyn had been involved in the fighting. Maverick had the feeling that Rune was going to act like her father for the rest of his days. He pulled a face at that, hoping it didn't mean that Rune was going to try to stop him from claiming her as his mate.

Rune's expression softened again. "I'm glad you're both safe. Let's get you out of here and close this place down for good."

Maverick released Bronwyn's hand and looked at her, right into her eyes, holding her gaze until he was sure she would remain close to him. He needed her by his side, needed to know at all times where she was and that she was safe.

"Head for Saint." Rune gestured towards the open side of the hangar where the big grizzly alpha was fighting alongside the cougar alpha, Rath.

Both dark-haired males blended with the night in their black clothing, illuminated only by the blaze of the helicopters and muzzle flashes as they exchanged fire with the hunters.

"You're coming too." Winnie's fear hit Maverick hard and he gave Rune a look that backed her up, because he didn't want her worrying about the black bear. He didn't want to worry about his friend either. He wanted Rune where he could see him, needed him to make it through this fight too.

"Not going anywhere." Rune gave her a soft look, one that revealed how deeply her concern had touched him, and gestured to her. "Come on. Wedge yourself between us."

She scooted around Maverick and shocked Rune by easing further away from cover to snag another gun. When she caught the look Rune was giving her, she looked at the weapon and then him and frowned.

"I can fight too. I'm not a cub anymore." A flush of heat touched her cheeks when she said that.

Rune slid him a knowing look, one that said Maverick was going to get a talking to about that later, once they were safely back home.

Maverick swallowed hard and followed Rune and Winnie, keeping low as he crossed an open stretch of concrete. He popped up from cover just long enough to sweep the room and locate a few hunters, and then gave Bronwyn a look that told her to stay put. She ignored him, rising to stand beside him and firing at the same time as he did.

Missing all her shots.

He had the feeling it was intentional, that his beautiful female still couldn't bring herself to harm someone, even when they were her enemy. She provided a distraction though, caused several hunters to panic, allowing him and Rune to pick them off. Their numbers were dwindling thanks to Knox and Lowe as they cut a path down one side of the hangar, and the cougar brothers who had teamed up to slice straight through the middle of it. Storm, Cobalt and Flint moved as one, the way they used cover, ducking behind it to pop up the second there was a break in hunter fire, making them look as if they had been trained for combat.

Maverick knew better though. The felines were employing their senses, using them to chart the position of every hunter in the hangar just as Maverick was. Only he was keeping tabs on those who were a danger to Bronwyn, his focus on getting her out of the hangar to safety as soon as possible.

Rune moved again and Maverick pushed Winnie, urging her to follow. She tucked her gun to her chest and hurried after the black bear, giving Maverick one hell of a view of her backside. The black fatigues she wore stretched tight over it, making him want to growl. Certainly made it impossible to keep his eyes off her.

She glanced back at him, a blush staining her cheeks even as she arched an eyebrow at him.

"Payback," he whispered with a wicked smile.

She had set him on fire by staring at his ass after all. It was only fair he got to stare at hers now their positions were reversed and he was following her.

They made it to the open side of the hangar just as the gunfire ceased.

Rune popped up and looked around, and Maverick eased to stand too.

"Think that was the last of them," Lowe hollered.

All of the tension drained from Maverick and he breathed a sigh as he looked at Winnie and then the others. A deep sense of gratitude rolled through him as the cougars and his pride slowly gathered around him. He would never be able to thank them enough for what they had done.

"What happened to your brother?" Saint said, his dark eyes soft as he frowned at Bronwyn.

She clammed up, her gaze falling to the ground.

Maverick stepped up beside her, was about to explain everything when she spoke.

"He's dead. He was never a captive. It was all a lie. He was helping the hunters… was running this place with them… and now he's dead." Her voice was soft, quiet, and she refused to look at anyone, even him, as everyone stared at her.

He shifted his hand closer to hers and brushed the back of it across her knuckles.

She glanced at him, tears lining her lashes, the pain he could feel in her immense, stealing his breath and filling him with a need to hold her.

Rune beat him to it, slung his arm around her and stroked her hair as she leaned into him, resting her head on his chest.

Making Maverick want to growl and snap fangs at his friend for daring to comfort his fated female. He dialled it back, told himself that Rune was happily mated and wasn't interested in stealing Winnie from him. Didn't stop him from wanting to punch the male.

"They made Maverick fight… they made me watch." She turned and buried her face against Rune's chest.

Rune growled and wrapped his arms around her, held her tightly as he flicked a look at Maverick.

"It was Klaus." Maverick couldn't take his eyes away from Bronwyn, couldn't stop himself from lifting a hand towards her as the pain he could feel in her grew more intense, and fear laced it. "I killed the son of a bitch."

Rune nodded. "Grace can be at peace now. I can be at peace. Thank you, brother."

Maverick shook his head, because he hadn't done it for Grace or for Rune. He had done it for his fated female, to protect her and keep her safe.

Rune gently gripped her shoulders and eased her back, gave Maverick another look that said they were going to have a talk about everything that had happened later, and then nodded and released her.

Maverick stepped up to her and gathered her into his arms, held her close to him, his heart drumming hard as she nestled against his chest and leaned her cheek against it, seeking comfort from him.

Knox jogged over to them with a canister of fuel in one hand and an RPG in the other.

He waggled both of them, his blue eyes bright with mischief. "Let's torch this place!"

Lowe rolled his eyes at his twin and so did Rath, but Storm and Flint grinned, looking more than up for it.

Maverick escorted Bronwyn outside, leaving the males to it, following Saint, Rath, Cobalt and Rune to a safe distance. As he turned back to face the hangar, he placed his arm around her shoulders, keeping her tucked close to him. Fire chased back the darkness, a series of explosions shaking the tarmac beneath his bare feet, and before long the entire compound was blazing.

As he watched it all burn, a strange sense of closure swept through him.

He was finally ready to let go of his past, because there was a future he wanted to seize with both hands.

He glanced at Bronwyn.

If she would have him.

CHAPTER 21

"You can stop glaring at me now." Maverick strode along the pebbly bank of the creek, the hot summer sunshine beating down on his bare back together with Rune's black look.

The big bear had caught up with him on his morning run and had been on his back ever since, dogging his every step and making it damned clear that he wasn't happy about what had happened with Bronwyn at the compound.

Last night, during a get together to celebrate taking down the Archangel compound, it had come out that he and Bronwyn had gotten physical, thanks to Skye and the other females interrogating her about the fact she kept blushing whenever she looked his way.

Rune had blown his top, causing a scene in front of the cougars. It had only been a matter of time before the bear had exploded, Maverick had known that from the second Rune had given him that look back in the hangar. He just wished his friend could have waited until they were alone in his cabin before he had come at him.

Maverick huffed. He knew in his heart that Rune meant well, was just being protective of Bronwyn, but gods, it stung a little. Rune knew the things he had been through, knew how low Maverick's opinion of himself could get, but it hadn't stopped the male from tossing it all out there in front of everyone.

"I came to apologise," Rune muttered behind him. "But I can see you're in about as good a mood as you were last night."

Maverick snorted. "I don't hear you apologising. All I hear is that bite in your tone that says you want another go at me."

He pivoted to face his friend, staring right into his pale blue eyes.

"So, come at me. Come on." He spread his arms wide and glared at Rune. "What are you waiting for? I'm sure there's someone within fifty miles who doesn't know how fucked up I am."

Rune heaved a sigh that stretched his black T-shirt tight across his chest and ran a hand over his close-cropped dark hair, a hint of guilt shining in his eyes now. "I'm sorry. I shouldn't have done that… I'd blame the beers, but… you know how I get about Winnie."

"Protective. Yeah. I get that." Maverick pivoted on his heel and began walking again, his steps harder now, each stride filled with anger and irritation, and despair. That last one ate away at him, chipping at his hope, and no matter how many times he told himself that Bronwyn had already known about the things he had done back when they were captives, he couldn't stop thinking she was going to leave and never look back. He snapped, "I know all about feeling protective when it comes to her."

Because part of him still wanted to protect her from himself.

And last night he had wanted to protect her from everyone who had given her looks that had made her grow awkward, had caused a blush to stain her cheeks that had looked an awful lot like shame to him.

She was ashamed of what they had done.

He growled and scrubbed a hand over his face, tried to tell that wretched, poisonous part of himself that was determined to make him feel as if he had lost her to shut up. It didn't. It whispered at him that he had ruined it all. He had destroyed the only thing he had ever really wanted in this world—a shot at forever with his beautiful fated female.

Maverick ground to a halt.

Stared at his feet as his shoulders sagged, all the hope bleeding from him as he thought about how quickly she had made an exit when Rune had launched into an argument with him. It was over before it had really begun. He should have seen that back in the hangar.

Only she had looked at him as if she loved him, as if she wanted forever with him too.

He curled his fingers into fists at his sides.

Maybe it had been the fear talking, the desperate desire to live. They had been about to die after all. Maybe he had mistaken regret for love.

"Mav," Rune murmured softly as he closed the distance between them.

Maverick sighed and closed his eyes, clenched his teeth so hard that his jaw flexed and then relaxed, on the verge of giving up even when part of him still wanted to fight, refused to let her go without trying to make her see that he could be worthy of her.

He just needed to do a little work on himself. Shape himself into someone better. Someone deserving of her love.

He just needed a chance.

He opened his eyes and looked at the grey pebbles. "I didn't want to do it."

Rune moved closer still, coming to stand beside him.

Before his friend could say anything, Maverick continued, "Winnie made the decision to do it. She knew what she was getting into. I tried so damned hard to protect her from that side of myself back then… but she saw it. She knew. She knew the kind of male I was… the kind of male I am."

Rune placed a hand on his right shoulder, his grip gentle. "Don't be so hard on yourself, Maverick."

"How am I supposed to be anything else?" He slid Rune a look. "Even my own friend thinks I'm a monster."

Rune's pale blue eyes narrowed as he frowned, his tone hardening. "I don't—"

Maverick shrugged free of his hold and refused to look at him, knew in his heart that Rune didn't think he was a monster. He was just acting out, fear that Bronwyn was going to leave him making him cranky.

"Just… I want to be alone," he muttered, even though what he really needed was to hear Rune tell him that he hadn't messed everything up, and that he wasn't a monster.

He needed some reassurance.

He took a few steps away from Rune and then stopped and looked back at him.

"I get it. You know? If it was someone else she wanted, I'd be feeling protective of her too. But I swear, Rune… I would never hurt her, and not because she's my fated one. I was blind back then, didn't see how I really felt about her, was in a dark place and didn't recognise her for the light she was in my life." He pressed his hand to his bare chest as he turned back to face Rune. His brow furrowed as he looked at his friend, aching inside. "But, gods, I need her. I've never loved anyone… but I love her. I love her, Rune… gods help her. I need her in my life. I need her as my mate. I just… need her. What can I do to make you see that? What can I say that will make you give me your permission?"

Rune's expression softened, his eyes warming. "You want my permission?"

Maverick cast his gaze down at his feet and then sighed and lifted it to lock with Rune's again as he ran his hand over his black hair. "I don't know. Maybe. Yes? I just… I don't want you angry with me. I want to know that you're cool with this thing happening between me and Bronwyn."

Rune stepped up to him, raised his hands and clasped both of Maverick's shoulders, his look earnest. "You don't need my permission."

"Kinda feels like I do." Maverick tried to smile, but it faltered as he thought about how Rune had reacted last night. "I want to claim Bronwyn. If she'll have me. Honestly, you're the closest thing to a parent she has. You're always acting like her dad. I don't want you mad at me for the rest of our lives. I'll be good to her. I tried to be good to her and she took the choice out of my hands… but I wasn't… It wasn't like back then… It was different with her."

Rune grimaced.

"This is verging on too much information. There's some things I don't need to know." Rune sighed and palmed Maverick's shoulders. "But… I'm not against you and Winnie. I'm not going to stand in the way. You say it was her choice. This should be her choice too. I hope she chooses you. You deserve to have something good happen to you… and I think Bronwyn would be good for you. I know you love her. I've always known. You're both as lousy as each other when it comes to hiding your feelings."

He patted Maverick's cheek, pulling a frown from him, and strolled past him.

Maverick looked over his shoulder, tracking Rune with his gaze as he headed towards the two cabins he and Maverick called home, lifting his hand to wave at Callie as his black-haired mate appeared between them.

What Rune had said felt as close to permission as Maverick was going to get.

He gazed at the cabin where Bronwyn was staying, nerves fluttering in his stomach as he thought about going to see her. Was she up yet? It was gone midday, but the drapes were still drawn. Maybe she was sleeping in late.

Maybe she was hiding from everyone.

From him.

He huffed and looked himself over, resisting the temptation to go to her and see if she was all right, and try to fix things. He was filthy from his run. Going to her now wouldn't make a great impression. And he wanted to make a good impression.

Rather than heading to her cabin, he strode towards his, running over what he would say to her. He would wash up, get everything he needed to tell her straight in his head, and then he would go to see her.

And hopefully she wouldn't turn him away.

Maverick took the steps up to his deck and then shoved the door open. He stepped inside, closed it behind him, and tossed his damp T-shirt on the dark grey couch that faced the log burner that stood against the wall to his left, his thoughts on Bronwyn. That look she had given him in the hangar was seared on his mind and he felt sure she had wanted to tell him that she loved him.

He filled the washbowl with water and cleaned himself off, debated heading to the outbuilding in the centre of the clearing to have a shower. It would probably be better than just rinsing off the sweat. He turned away from the kitchen that overlooked the deck and frowned as he headed for the far end of the cabin, to the navy terrycloth robe hung by the wardrobe there.

The door behind him opened.

Maverick huffed as he reached for the robe. "If you've come to lecture me again or you changed your mind about what you said, I'm not going to listen. I love Winnie and I want to be with her. I'll be a good male for her. I know I will… or I hope I will."

"I know you will."

That soft female voice wasn't the one he had been expecting to hear.

He pivoted on his heel to face Bronwyn where she stood by the door, an awkward edge to her honey-coloured eyes as she fidgeted with the hem of her burgundy flowing camisole.

His cheeks heated as he gazed at her and hers coloured too as she smiled nervously.

"Rune read you the riot act too?" she said softly, warmth in her eyes as her brow furrowed slightly. "I got the whole speech this morning. He came to check on me and bring me coffee, and ended up trying to convince me to take things slowly and lecturing me on not getting caught up in the moment… that a bond was forever. Like I don't know that."

Maverick scowled at that and scoffed. "He can hardly talk. He knew his wolf for all of five minutes before he was mating with her, claiming her as his forever."

Her smile wobbled a little, her nerves showing in it. "And we've known each other for a long time. Spent years together. You're right. He can't really lecture us. Besides… I didn't listen to a word he had to say."

That smile grew a little mischievous.

Maverick shook his head and sighed. "Guessing I'm not the only one who took his meddling badly and put him in his place."

She shrugged. "I love Rune, but honestly… this thing happening between us has nothing to do with him. This is our decision to make… and I thought about—was up all night thinking about it and wanted to come here so many times to talk to you about it. When I finally plucked up the courage, you were out running. Are you feeling better?"

"No." He loved the way she smiled as he issued that flat and blunt answer. "Not sure I'm going to feel better until I know… Bronwyn… I love you. I've never loved anyone… not the way I love you. I need to know… will you be my mate?"

Her smile softened again. "Yes! Yes. A thousand times, yes. I want to be your mate. More than anything, Maverick. I love you too… with all my heart."

He closed the distance between them in a handful of strides. His heart surged in his chest as he swept her into his arms, as he claimed her lips in a soft kiss that had warmth rolling through him. That warmth turned to heat as she wrapped her arms around his neck and held him to her, as her lips danced across his and their hearts raced in time with each other.

Maverick pulled back, gripping her by her backside, holding her with her feet suspended off the ground. He searched her eyes, seeking out even the barest trace of uncertainty.

"You're sure about this? Rune is right. This is forever. Once I claim you, I'm never letting you go."

She lifted her right hand and stroked her fingers through his black hair, twining it around their tips and teasing him with that light touch. "And if I said fine, let's not do this, you'd just let me go?"

"Hell, no. I'm never letting you go. I need you too much. I love you too much. Even if it took me forever to convince you I'll make a good mate for you, to make you love me as deeply as I love you, I wouldn't stop. I wouldn't let you go. I can't." Did he look as desperate as he felt and sounded as he gazed at her?

The warmth that filled her eyes said that he did and that she liked it.

She dropped her hand and lightly caressed his cheek. "I don't think you could make me love you any more than I already do, Maverick. I've loved you from afar for decades… feel as if I've been waiting for this moment my whole life. I don't want to wait any longer."

Gods.

This female had his heart surging all over again, pride swelling within his chest as he gazed at her and saw she meant every word that left her lips. He had never felt so loved, so blessed.

He claimed her lips again, his kiss harder this time, the primal instinct to bend her to his will rising to the fore as he thought about where this kiss would lead.

Bronwyn would finally be his.

But they were going to do things right this time.

Maverick carried her up to his loft bedroom and gently set her down on the dark covers. He slowly stripped her, savoured revealing her to his hungry eyes and the heat that bloomed in her gaze as she watched him. Awareness swept through him as he eased back onto his knees by her feet, as he locked gazes with her. Her eyes shone with that same awareness, with the need that rolled through him too, had him aching for her.

He stepped off the bed and stripped off his sweatpants, kicked them away and growled as Bronwyn teased him by stroking the fingers of her right hand down the valley between her breasts, sending his temperature soaring to that of the sun. She smiled, a wicked edge to it that tore a groan from him together with how she trailed her fingers lower, drawing his gaze down with them.

Unable to resist her siren song any longer, he crawled onto the bed and covered her, kissed her hard as her soft body cushioned his. He groaned again as her legs parted to accommodate him and he nestled between them, her heat meeting his throbbing shaft. He couldn't stop himself from grinding against her to tease her, relished her soft moan and how she arched into him, seeking more contact with him.

Her nails scored his nape, sending a shudder down his spine and pleasure sweeping through him as his eyes slipped shut. His fangs lengthened in response, his cock growing harder as his primal instincts tried to steal control. He leashed them and held them back, rolled with her so she was on top of him, submitting to her.

A blush bloomed on her cheeks as she gazed down at him, heat turning her eyes golden as she raked them over him, as she pressed her palms to his chest and swept them over his pectorals. Her teeth teased her lower lip as she caressed and stroked him, maddening him and cranking up his need of her.

He reached his hands above his head and buried them under the pillow, caging them there, drawing a low moan from Bronwyn as her face crumpled, desire flashing across it.

"You don't know—" She cut herself off, nerves flickering in her eyes to replace the heat as she cast her gaze down at her hands, avoiding him.

"Don't know what?" he husked, his voice gravelly and low with the desire she roused in him, the fierce need he was battling to control. He wanted to seize hold of her and kiss her, wanted to bend her to his will, but he also wanted this moment to be perfect.

And the best way to make that happen was to let her be in control.

She nibbled her lower lip, leaned over him and shattered his ability to think as her breasts brushed his stomach and her lips teased his chest. He groaned and forgot what he had wanted to know, forgot everything including his name as she swirled her tongue around his nipple and then raked her short nails over his stomach. Gods.

He tightened his grip on the pillow.

Bronwyn breathed against his chest, "I've dreamed of doing this so many times."

He stilled. "You have?"

He craned his neck and gazed down at her, but she refused to look at him, kept hiding in maddening him with licks and swirls of her tongue.

"With me?" He really needed to know the answer to that question.

Her shy glance said it all.

She had dreamed of him, a lot of times judging by how red her cheeks were, how she could barely hold his gaze for a second before looking away from him. She didn't need to be shy about this. She didn't need to feel awkward.

He loved that she had dreamed of him.

"Was it always like this?" He relaxed into the mattress, shivered as she lightly scored her nails down his sides and shuffled backwards.

His mind dived down wicked routes involving her mouth and his shaft.

"No." She pressed kisses around his navel and then downwards and his cock kicked, eager for her to reach it. "Most of the time it was like… it was like at the compound."

He frowned.

Opened his mouth to ask her whether she was serious and she had fantasised about him taking her like that.

Lost his ability to talk as she wrapped her lips around his hard length, her heat encasing him, her soft wetness driving him out of his mind. He groaned and fought the urge to rock into her mouth as she tentatively explored him, as she teased the shaft with her fingers and the head with her tongue.

Oh gods.

He couldn't remember ever being on the receiving end of something like this. He had never been the submissive one and found that he not only liked it—he loved it. He loved how she teased him, how she moaned when he did, as if she took pleasure in making him feel good. She wrapped her fingers around him and sucked, and he damn near came.

Maverick tunnelled his fingers into her chestnut hair and pulled her up to him, claimed her mouth in a bruising kiss as need collided with what she had told him about her dreams, stoking his hunger for her.

She gripped his shoulder and rolled onto her back, taking him with her, and he groaned as he pressed between her thighs, rocked his length along her slick heat and thought about being inside her. She skimmed her hand down his spine and over his hip, reached between them and gripped his shaft.

"I need this." Her whispered confession hit him hard.

Had him drawing back and taking over from her, gripping himself and easing downwards. He couldn't hold back the groan that rolled up his throat as he inched into her, slowly joining them, savouring it this time. She moaned with him, arched to press her chest to his and clutched his shoulders as he filled her.

Maverick stilled and gazed down at her when he was as deep as he could go, stared into her eyes and felt connected to her in a way he had never experienced before. She lifted her hands from his shoulders and framed his face, drew him down to her and kissed him. He groaned and stole control of the kiss as he moved inside her, taking things slowly this time, drawing it out and making love with her.

Primal instinct demanded he dominate her and take her harder, but he held it back, refusing to succumb to it. It would take control at some point, but for now, he was going to savour this moment. Her kiss was sweet as he moved inside her, long strokes that had her moaning in his arms, arching and pleading him for more. He dropped his left hand to her hip and held her in place, stopping her from writhing and pushing at his control. She moaned again, driving him on as she deepened the kiss, as she raised her knees and wrapped her legs around him. He rocked into her, each meeting of their hips bliss to him, the gentle pace of their lovemaking unravelling him, warming him to his bones.

Making him aware of how deeply he loved her.

And how deeply she loved him.

He drew back, resting on his right elbow, and she opened her eyes and locked gazes with him. Everything felt more intense the moment their gazes collided, as he fell into her golden eyes and all the love they held wrapped around him. Her eyes grew hooded and she moaned and arched off the mattress, her head tipping back as her body quivered around his, clenching and unclenching him.

Maverick followed her over the edge, groaned as release surged through him, the intensity of it robbing him of breath and making him feel hazy. He had never experienced something so incredible, so overwhelming and beautiful.

A blush stained her cheeks as she gazed up at him, her eyes hazy and filled with the pleasure he could feel in her.

"Claim me. I want to be yours forever." Those words undid him, stole his heart all over again, and he couldn't stop himself.

He withdrew from her, flipped her onto her front and impaled her again, relishing her sweet cry as he filled her.

She moaned as he grabbed her and pulled her up to him, so she was sitting on his thighs, his length buried deep inside her. When she ran her fingers through her hair and pulled it away from her nape, he wanted to growl and not only because the urge to sink his fangs into her grew stronger.

The tiny 657-B tattooed low on her neck held his gaze—the mark the hunters had given her when they had captured her. A number that was around four-hundred-and-thirty higher than his own.

They had survived hell, had been put to the test so many times, and had endured it all, emerging from it with scars on their souls and hope for a brighter future.

One Maverick had never dared to dream would be his.

But now it was right here in his arms.

And he wanted it with all his heart—the heart that belonged to her.

"Don't keep me waiting," Bronwyn whispered. "You promised me forever."

Maverick kept his promise.

He sank his fangs into her nape.

Claiming her as his mate.

As his forever.

The End

ABOUT THE AUTHOR

Felicity Heaton is a New York Times and USA Today best-selling author who writes passionate paranormal romance books. In her books she creates detailed worlds, twisting plots, mind-blowing action, intense emotion and heart-stopping romances with leading men that vary from dark deadly vampires to sexy shape-shifters and wicked werewolves, to sinful angels and hot demons!

If you're a fan of paranormal romance authors Lara Adrian, J R Ward, Sherrilyn Kenyon, Kresley Cole, Gena Showalter, Larissa Ione and Christine Feehan then you will enjoy her books too.

If you love your angels a little dark and wicked, her best-selling Her Angel romance series is for you. If you like strong, powerful, and dark vampires then try the Vampires Realm romance series or any of her stand alone vampire romance books. If you're looking for vampire romances that are sinful, passionate and erotic then try her London Vampires romance series. Or if you like hot-blooded alpha heroes who will let nothing stand in the way of them claiming their destined woman then try her Eternal Mates series. It's packed with sexy heroes in a world populated by elves, vampires, fae, demons, shifters, and more. If sexy Greek gods with incredible powers battling to save our world and their home in the Underworld are more your thing, then be sure to step into the world of Guardians of Hades.

If you have enjoyed this story, please take a moment to contact the author at **author@felicityheaton.com** or to post a review of the book online

Connect with Felicity:
Website – http://www.felicityheaton.com
Blog – http://www.felicityheaton.com/blog/
Twitter – http://twitter.com/felicityheaton
Facebook – http://www.facebook.com/felicityheaton
Goodreads – http://www.goodreads.com/felicityheaton
Mailing List – http://www.felicityheaton.com/newsletter.php

FIND OUT MORE ABOUT HER BOOKS AT:
http://www.felicityheaton.com

Made in the USA
Coppell, TX
22 February 2024

29295974R00111